25
THE GIRLS OF CANBY HALL

THE GHOST OF CANBY HALL

EMILY CHASE

SCHOLASTIC INC.
New York Toronto London Auckland Sydney

ISBN 0-590-41090-3

12 11 10 9 8 7 6 5 4 3 2 1   7 8 9/8 0 1 2/9

Printed in the U.S.A.   01

First Scholastic printing, December 1987

THE GIRLS
OF CANBY HALL

25

THE GHOST OF
CANBY HALL

THE GIRLS OF CANBY HALL

CHAPTER ONE

"Spring is so gorgeous here in New England!" October Houston told Jane Barrett for the forty-second time in as many days. "I mean, Texas is nice, too," speaking loyally of her home state, "but the desert doesn't spring to life in the same way. Massachusetts is just so . . . green!" Tall and lanky, wearing jeans and a short-sleeved plaid blouse, her wavy red hair held back by combs, Toby gazed happily around the Canby Hall campus. "I love the way those huge, old trees get all lacey with new blossoms. They look like the curtains at my grandmother's house."

"Why, Toby!" Jane exclaimed with a grin, "that's positively poetic! I didn't know you had it in you. I thought *I* was the literary one." The two girls were a study in contrast. Toby's shirt had slipped out of the waistband of her jeans, little tendrils of hair escaped from the combs, and her cheeks were flushed

1

from the warmth of a late-spring day, while Jane's perfectly tanned face remained composed, her blonde hair unruffled, her white jumpsuit fresh and unwrinkled.

Toby returned Jane's grin. "Aw, shucks, Miz Barrett," she said in an exaggerated drawl, " 'twarn't nothin'. Easy as rollin' off a greased log."

Jane laughed. Toby was a rancher's daughter from Texas, and she and Jane, who was from Boston, and their roommate, Andrea Cord, who was from Chicago, were all as unalike as their accents. The differences had caused problems at first, but now the three girls were close friends, able to appreciate — and laugh at — those differences.

Right now, Jane agreed heartily with Toby's appraisal of their New England spring. If one had to attend a private school, and according to her parents, one certainly *did*, she was glad she'd chosen Canby Hall, which generations of her family had attended. The lovely old campus wore its new green coat well. The lawn, always meticulously maintained, surrounded the antique brick buildings with a smooth velvet carpet. The ivy on the walls of Main Building had sprung to new life and the water in the pond sparkled under a late May sun. And Toby was right about the trees. Although they didn't have lace curtains like this in the Barretts' Boston mansion, Jane certainly knew what Toby meant. The blossoms and baby leaves that hung over them as they walked across campus really did look like a sort of delicate green lace.

"Spring comes really late here," she told Toby, "but it's worth the wait. I never can figure out if that's because it really is so pretty or just because winter is so terrible."

Laughing, they entered the dining hall.

Their roommate was waiting for them. Andy, slender and lithe like the dancer she was, enjoyed the beautiful spring weather as much as Toby. It was an appreciation, Andy said, developed by her native Chicago's legendary bad winters. Sitting at a long table near a window, she was staring out at the fresh green campus, long brown fingers twirling her short, dark hair. What a year it had been! Not only had her roommates traveled with her to her home in Chicago, where Toby and Jane had actually helped out in the Cord family restaurant, she, Andrea Cord, had slept overnight in the Barrett mansion in Boston. Andy giggled softly, remembering both Jane's struggles as a temporary waitress and Toby's confrontations with high society. It still amazed her that they'd conquered all of their differences and their problems and were now good friends.

Andy shifted impatiently in her seat as the

dining hall began to fill up. Lunch on a Saturday wasn't usually this busy. Students often headed for town on Saturdays to shop or take in a movie. But finals were rapidly approaching and most of this weekend would be spent on campus, poring over notebooks and textbooks.

Where were Toby and Jane? Andy'd left Baker early to drop off some books at the library and pick up more for her history term paper. But they should be here by now. Jane was so pokey. . . .

But Andy understood Jane a lot better now that she'd actually spent some time in the Barrett mansion — where finger bowls were used at every evening meal! Andy laughed, remembering, as she spotted her roommates in the doorway. Everything in Jane's world was so very proper, so well-ordered. Maybe being late for things was just Jane's own way of rebelling against all that order. Or maybe, Andy thought dryly, Jane just hasn't yet accepted that the world doesn't operate on her time schedule. That sounds more like our Jane.

Watching Toby's free and easy stride as she approached the table, Andy thought that Toby had probably learned more than any of them this past year. She had confided in Andy after that weekend in Boston that she and her father seldom used a tablecloth at meals in the ranch house, relying on place mats instead. And the ranch table had never held anything as exotic as a finger bowl. Andy and Toby had had a good laugh over that.

Yes, it had certainly been an interesting year.

"Hi, guys," she said cheerfully as her roommates arrived. " 'Bout time! What'd you do, come by way of Boston?"

"We just took our time, that's all," Jane answered loftily. "In case you haven't noticed, it's a real knockout day out there. We wanted to enjoy the wonders of Mother Nature."

Andy snorted good-naturedly. "You mean you wanted to improve your tan. Me, I come tanned." Initially sensitive about being part of a distinct minority on the Canby Hall campus, she now felt very comfortable and could even joke about it. "C'mon, let's eat. I'm starved!"

"You're always starved," Jane retorted. "It's a good thing your parents own a restaurant."

They chose hot dogs because, as Toby put it, the tuna fish looked "suspicious." They were returning to their table, trays in hand, when Penny Vanderark stopped them. A small, compact girl in jeans and a blue T-shirt, her blue eyes sparkled with excitement, and her fair cheeks were flushed.

"Guess what, Jane?" she cried, putting a

hand on Jane's arm. "Guess who's got a really good chance of walking away with the Literature Award for our class?"

"I haven't the foggiest idea," Jane replied coolly, although everyone in school knew Jane's ambition was to be a writer. They also knew that Jane Barrett's best subject was English Literature. "You?" Although Penny wasn't as accomplished a student as Jane, she was a gifted writer and had had some of her material published in the school literary journal.

"Well, yes," Penny admitted, blushing, "I *am* in the running, according to rumor, anyway. But *you* are, too. Isn't that great? That's what I wanted to tell you. I'm sure you'll get it."

"Jane!" Andy and Toby called in unison, "That's great! Congratulations! And you, too, Penny."

Penny grinned, while Jane just smiled and moved toward the table. "I haven't won anything yet," she reminded them as they all sat down. She glanced over at Penny as she opened her milk carton. "Aren't there usually three nominees?"

Penny nodded. "Yeah. The other one is someone with a French name, I think. Fifi or Gigi, something like that? Got any idea who that might be?"

The three roommates exchanged glances. "Not Gigi," Jane said, "tell me it's not Gigi!"

She looked at Andy. "Maybe it really *is* a Fifi?"

"Jane. There *is* no Fifi at Canby Hall. There's only a Gigi. Gigi Norton."

"No. It can't be her. She's not just a pain in the neck, she's not even very bright. How could it be her?"

"She's bright enough in English," Andy said calmly, picking up her hot dog. "She does something important on the school paper. I've seen a couple of editorials written by her. They were sort of whiny, which should surprise no one, but they weren't bad."

Penny's blue eyes widened. "You know her?" Relatively new to Canby Hall, her circle of acquaintances was narrower than theirs.

Toby made a face. "Yeah, we know her. Being around her is about as much fun as stepping on a porcupine."

"What's wrong with her?"

Andy waved a hand in dismissal. "Let's not talk about her, okay? It'll ruin my appetite." She bit into her hot dog. Mustard oozed out of the bun and plopped onto her plate. "Let's just say if you tell Gigi it's a nice day, she'll say it's probably going to rain."

"It's not that she's an ax-murderer," Jane explained. "Not as far as we *know*, anyway. She's just — "

"Enough, already!" Andy cried. "As long as that Norton person is the topic of conversation at this table, I will *not* be able to eat."

"That'll be the day," Jane commented. But she was perfectly willing to change the subject. "So," she asked Penny, "are we going to have to do something boring like write essays? Don't they assign something like that when there are three competitors for the same award?"

Penny groaned and shook her head. "I don't know, but I certainly hope not. I don't have *time* to write an essay! I'm never going to pass a single subject except English, I just know it."

"Don't be silly," Jane said, wiping her mouth daintily with her paper napkin. "We girls from Baker Hall don't fail subjects. That's ridiculous."

Penny stared at her, but Andy and Toby laughed. "Relax, Penny," Andy said quickly. "Nothing horrid will happen to you if you should happen to fail something like geometry, for instance. But you probably won't. And even if you do, I promise you can go on living in Baker Hall, anyway."

Penny looked relieved, while Jane looked skeptical, as though she herself might see to it that Penny would be banished from Baker should she pull an F in any subject.

"Speaking of bad news," Toby said quietly. "There's Gigi Norton now. She just joined the food line."

"Probably after her daily ration of eye of

newt and tail of toad," Andy said. "No doubt her cauldron is empty."

"That's her?" Penny asked. "Then I do know her. She's in my art class. She always hates everyone else's work. Always has a sly little comment designed to hurt someone's feelings. I did this neat drawing of my brother Jason. It really looked a lot like him. And she asked me if it was a picture of my pet! Said he looked like a poodle. Can you believe it?"

"I don't know," Andy said seriously. "I've never seen your brother."

Penny laughed and stood up. "I have to go get something to eat, or I'm going to pass out and land on the floor. I don't want to get demerits for cluttering up the dining hall, so excuse me, please. Save my seat, okay?"

"She's so cute," Jane said, as Penny joined the food line behind Gigi Norton.

"And *you're* so smart," Andy told Jane. "It just knocks me out that you're up for the Lit Award. Aren't you excited? Just think, Room 407 can walk away with a major award at that dinner."

Jane's tanned skin deepened in color. "Well, Penny's up for it, too, don't forget. And we all know what a terrific writer she is."

"She's not as good as you," Toby said loyally.

"If you have an essay to write," Andy

pointed out, "you're going to be really cramped for time, what with finals, too. You're not going to have much free time."

"Oh, I get it," Jane said in a voice full of mock injury, "I do all the work and you guys bask in the reflected glory."

"You got it!" Andy agreed, laughing. "That's the way it works. Ain't it great?"

Jane wasn't really annoyed. She was too happy about the news. The Lit Award! Did she really have a chance at it? Everyone would be at the Awards Banquet and if she won, her parents would be invited, too. Families of the major award winners were always invited. Wouldn't they be proud? And it could definitely help when her father began his argument that investment banking was a great career choice for her. Journalism was her own choice, and this award could help convince him that she was right. It certainly couldn't hurt.

Gigi Norton interrupted Jane's daydreams. "So," she said, standing behind Jane, tray in hand, "not practicing your acceptance speech, are you, Barrett?"

Startled, Jane looked up. "What? No, Gigi. And you shouldn't be, either. Penny is a fantastic writer."

A tall girl with pale skin and lifeless dark hair, Gigi made a face. "That airhead! She's no threat to anyone."

"When she has a pen in her hand, she is,"

Jane said firmly. "She's had material printed in *The Canby Hall Journal*."

The sneer remained. "So have I. Forget Penny, Barrett. This contest is between you and me, and you know it. Just don't bother with an acceptance speech. Waste of time, if you ask me."

"I don't remember asking you," Jane replied, her voice cool. "Go away, Gigi. Go find a broom to test-ride."

Unable to think of a response, Gigi turned away angrily just as Penny arrived with her tray.

"What did *she* want?" Penny asked as she sat down.

Jane shrugged. "Nothing important. Just warning you and me that she intends to win that award. You can see how shaken up I am."

Unperturbed, Penny said, "Well, you guys sure have her pegged. When we were on line, I told her I thought it was a gorgeous day. Guess what she said?"

The occupants of Room 407 exchanged glances before saying in one voice, "Looks like rain to me."

"Right!" Penny declared with a grin.

They all laughed.

CHAPTER TWO

When they returned to Room 407, they found a note from their housemother, Meredith, tacked to the door. "Stopped by to say hi," was all it said.

"Let's go up to her penthouse and say 'hi' back," Andy suggested.

"Anything to put off studying!" Toby agreed.

Meredith's "penthouse" was on the top floor. Any student who felt a need to climb the stairs and cry on a comforting shoulder or confide a secret was always welcome. A summons usually meant Meredith's concern over falling grades or disciplinary action for an infraction of Canby Hall's rules. Really major infractions were referred to Patrice Allardyce, Canby's tall, authoritative, nononsense headmistress.

Meredith's dark, straight hair was pulled back into a ponytail and fastened with a brass butterfly. She was wearing a beige skirt unbuttoned down the front over white shorts and a white T-shirt, and she had a tennis racket in her hand.

"Hi," Meredith said cheerfully as she greeted them at the door. "I have some news. Canby Hall has received a delightful gift — several items from an estate in England, items that once belonged to young Julia Canby, for whom the school was founded. You remember — Horace Canby's thirteen-year-old daughter?

Jane nodded. "She died very young, I remember that. Of a fever or pneumonia, something like that?"

Meredith nodded. "Yes, a fever. She was visiting relatives in Europe at the time. The items we just received are from that estate. I haven't seen the things myself yet, but according to Ms. Allardyce, one item in particular, a music box, is quite lovely. And I believe there is a diary and, I think, some letters. Everything is on display in the library. Because they're very old and fragile, you won't be allowed to check them out. But you can certainly enjoy them there."

No one said anything. Disappointed in their lack of enthusiasm, Meredith added, "Won't it be interesting to see things like this from another century, things that mean something in the history of Canby Hall?"

"Well, sure," Andy said, looking doubtful. "I guess. But that was all so long ago."

"Well, *I* think it sounds fascinating," Jane said.

Toby nodded slowly. "Maybe we could go see the exhibit now. We were going to the library to study for finals, anyway. We can take a few minutes to see that music box."

"*And* the diary," Jane said, beginning to feel excitement. A diary from 1897! When would she ever have another chance like this?

Meredith smiled her approval. "Well, great!" she said, leaving them at the door. "I'll probably head over myself in a little while. I'm anxious to see the display, too."

As they made their way back across campus, Andy said grumpily, "I expected her to say something about the Lit Award. Think she doesn't know about it?"

"Of course she knows," Jane snapped. "Everyone else does. Why wouldn't she?" Then she added more calmly, "Relax, Andy. Penny lives in this building, too. It wouldn't be right for Meredith to play favorites."

"Who said anything about playing favorites? I just thought she could have wished you luck." Andy giggled. "Maybe she thinks you're the one person who doesn't need it."

That thought brightened Jane considerably. "C'mon, here's the library. I'm dying to see Julia Canby's things. I'll bet they're really nice. Her family was rich, you know."

Andy's eyes widened. "No kidding? Gee, I thought Horace Canby bought all of this land with trading stamps or coupons."

A well-placed elbow in her ribs sent her into giggles again. "I don't see," she gasped as they hurried up the library stairs, "what's so exciting about a bunch of old papers?"

"And a music box," Toby reminded her. "Don't forget the music box. That sounds interesting."

Although Andy continued to grumble, she allowed herself to be propelled along.

"You know, lots of people are interested in historical things," Jane teased Andy. "*You're* the oddball."

Andy looked indignant. "I'm no oddball! *Some* people just want an excuse to quit studying for a while, that's all. They probably couldn't care less about Julia Canby's musty old things."

Jane knew Andy probably had a point. *Everyone* was sick of staring at textbooks until the figures and letters blurred. And Jane herself was grateful for a reason to avoid straining her brain, even for a little while. But she was also excited about the display. And she was sure there were at least a few other students who felt the same way. Andy just wasn't one of them.

Sure enough, inside the library a crowd had already gathered around a glass case on a high table in the center of the main reading room. Soft "oohs" and "aahs" drifted above the exhibit.

Jane tried to edge in closer, but the crowd formed one solid wall. She tapped her foot impatiently.

"Relax!" Andy scolded. "I just can't deal with your rush to see musty old relics from the Victorian age."

Jane ignored her and continued to push gently at the wall until she made a hole for herself as others departed. Andy and Toby stayed close to her and finally, they all found a spot with an unobstructed view of the exhibit.

The gifts sat on a square of blue velvet. The center spot was occupied by Julia Canby's music box. Fashioned of fine porcelain in a creamy ivory, its lid was adorned with a porcelain ice skater fully dressed in Victorian clothes: a deep blue velvet full-length coat with a nipped-in waist and a full, billowing skirt. She was wearing black skates and carrying a white fur muff. Toby, who had been introduced to ice-skating during the past winter on the Canby Hall pond, was enchanted with the music box. "Isn't it beautiful!" she breathed, her eyes shining. "Isn't it just the prettiest thing you ever saw!"

Jane was much more interested in the little diary. Bound in soft, smooth, dark leather and fastened with a tarnished gold clasp, it seemed to call out to her. "Secrets!" she almost heard it say, "I have wonderful secrets from the past!"

"I can't wait to get my hands on that!" she whispered to Andy. "And those letters, too." The letters were bound in faded blue ribbon and the envelope sitting on top of the packet looked as fragile as tissue paper.

Andy sniffed with disdain. "They're not even written by Julia Canby," she pointed out unnecessarily. "Look, they're addressed *to* her. I thought you wanted to learn about *her*. Shouldn't you have letters written *by* her for that?"

"Andy," Jane said patiently, "if Julia wrote letters to people and mailed them, they would no longer belong to her, would they? They'd belong to the people who received them in the mail. So how would they become a part of this exhibit? These are things that belonged to *her*. And I *will* learn something about her from these letters. You can learn a lot about a person from letters written to them."

Andy just sniffed again. She shifted impatiently from one foot to the other, anxious to return to the beautiful day outside.

"I wonder what tune that music box plays," Toby mused aloud.

One of the librarians, Ms. Freer, came up behind them just then. The crowd had all but disappeared. "You can take the box out, Toby," she said. "It's okay. You just can't take it from the library. And you must handle it gently, of course. It's very old and very fragile."

Toby's tanned face went a shade paler. "What if I drop it?"

Ms. Freer laughed. "You won't drop it. But if it'll make you feel better, I'll hold it. I'd like to hear the melody, too."

Lifting the lid on the glass case, she reached in and carefully removed the music box from its resting place. At the same time, an eager Jane picked up the diary, leaving the packet of letters for another time. The librarian gently deposited the music box on a long, narrow table. "You lift the lid, Toby," she urged, smiling.

With wonder in her blue eyes, Toby slowly, carefully, lifted the lid. Inside the box stood a miniature replica of the Victorian skater on the outside of the lid. "Oh," Toby breathed, "look at that! Isn't that just amazing!"

Even Andy looked impressed. "It must fold down when you close the lid. I have one at home that has a ballerina inside."

The musical strains that tinkled from the box were familiar. "It's 'The Skaters Waltz.' " Toby said. "Well, that makes sense, doesn't it?"

"Yeah," Andy said dryly. "Somehow, I just don't think 'Home, Home On The Range' would have worked, do you?"

"Oh, Andy," Jane said, "stop trying so hard to be cool. You know you love it!"

As enchanted by the music box as Jane was, she felt as if the diary was burning a hole through her palms. She couldn't help wishing she could take it outside and sit under one of the big old elm trees, where she could lose herself in Julia Canby's words. But beautiful day or not, she couldn't wait another second to open the pretty little diary.

"I'm going to find a quiet corner and see what life was like in the nineteenth century," she told the others. "Okay, Ms. Freer?"

Ms. Freer glanced around the library. It had emptied out. No one but Jane was willing to give up the pleasures of a New England spring day. "Sure, I guess so. You seem to be the only one interested in being cooped up inside on a day like this. But if someone comes in to see the exhibit, be sure and share the diary with them, okay?"

Jane frowned. She already felt a strong sense of ownership toward the diary. But it *wasn't* hers, and she knew the gifts had been intended for all of the students. "Sure," she agreed. But she couldn't help hoping with all her might that no one would come looking for the little book.

"You're nuts!" Andy said as Jane moved away. "You're going to lose that tan you've been working on because of an old book? You'll go back to Boston pale as a ghost!"

Jane shrugged. She found a chair next to a window and made herself comfortable. Then she opened the leather diary. And from the very first line on the very first page, Jane became entranced.

February 7, 1897.
Dear Diary,
    London is surely the most exciting city in the whole world! If only Papa would let me go exploring. But he insists that Mathilde keep her eagle eye on me at all times. He treats me like a child!

Figuring quickly in her head, Jane smiled. Julia Canby had been all of thirteen years old when she wrote that entry. Jane fingered the delicate paper thoughtfully. The motion made a crinkling sound that echoed throughout the now-silent library. In those days, she reminded herself, women didn't live as long as they do now. That's why they married at a much younger age, sometimes as young as fourteen. So maybe it made sense that Julia Canby felt that she was being treated like a child.

    How I yearn to explore this exciting and wondrous city on my own, but it shall never happen. I must content myself with Mathilde's idea of entertainment, mostly stuffy museums and monuments, and those only in the light of day.

Jane made a face. Poor Julia! Whoever Mathilde was, she didn't sound like much fun. Probably some sort of governess.

How exciting London must be at night! I must conspire to persuade Papa to accompany me to an evening concert or to a fine restaurant. If only I can, dear Diary.

Jane sighed sympathetically and turned the page.

CHAPTER THREE

That night at dinner, everyone talked about the Literature Award. Andy noticed Gigi Norton glaring in their direction as one student after another wished Penny and Jane good luck. Few girls, if any, included Gigi in their good wishes. Andy might have felt a pang of sympathy for her neglected classmate if Gigi hadn't had such a long history of rotten behavior.

"You know," Gigi finally called out in an annoyed voice, "no one has *won* that award yet. I think you're all jumping the gun huddling around Barrett that way. Anything can happen between now and the night of the dinner." And with that, she stood up and stalked out of the room.

"Well!" Penny exclaimed with a grin, "I guess she told *us*! Do we all feel properly chastened?"

Jane's eyebrows shot up. "Chastened? No

wonder you're up for the award, using a word like chastened." Penny laughed.

"I don't think you guys should be joking about this," Andy warned. "I don't trust Gigi. She wants that award, a lot. I don't think *I'd* want to be her competition."

"Well, you're not," Jane replied lightly. "So relax! What can she do, anyway? This isn't an athletic competition. If she sneaks up behind me and pushes me down the stairs and breaks my leg in two places, I can still write that essay."

"Just don't take Gigi too lightly, that's all I'm saying," Andy said firmly. "C'mon, let's go call Oakley and find out what the guys are doing." Oakley Prep was a nearby boys' school. Both Andy's boyfriend, Matt Hall, and Jane's, a boy named Cary Slade, were students there.

Jane shook her head. "Count me out. Finals are creeping up on me like poison ivy, and I can't let Cary Slade's gorgeous smile distract me."

Andy's dark eyes narrowed suspiciously. "Are you *really* going to study? Or are you just in a hurry to get back to that silly old diary?"

"That silly old diary, for your information," Jane snapped, jumping up, "is a treasure of great historical value."

Andy gave a hoot.

Jane's cheeks flamed angrily. "And considering that you pulled the lowest grade in

Room 407 in history last term, it wouldn't hurt you to take a look at that diary."

"It was a B minus," Andy corrected hotly. "And it would have been a B if I hadn't fouled up on the date of Sherman's march through Georgia. And I suppose Julia Canby was hanging out in Atlanta during the Civil War?"

"Oh, you're hopeless!" Jane said in exasperation. "I'm going to the library. See you later." She picked up her tray and left.

Andy turned to Toby. "How about you, roomie? You up for some fun?"

Toby groaned and shook her head. "No can do. That geometry final is going to be my Alamo if I don't cozy up to my notes tonight. Planes, angles, I just can't get the hang of that stuff. Sorry, Andy." And she got up and followed Jane out of the dining hall.

To Andy's disappointment, Matt was studying, too. When she called to see if he'd take in a movie in town with her, he reluctantly declined. "We could study together, though," he offered, hope in his voice. "I could come over there."

Andy frowned and made a face. "You know better than that," she said softly. "I can't concentrate when you're sitting across the table from me." He laughed, but she sighed heavily. "What a rotten way to spend a Saturday night, especially a beautiful spring night!"

"Yeah, well, it's just that time of year.

When finals are over, I promise I'll take you out and we'll celebrate. But if I don't hit the books tonight, there won't be anything *to* celebrate. Maybe I can get over there tomorrow, okay?"

Andy hung up and then realized she hadn't told Matt about the Julia Canby exhibit. Oh, well, why would he be any more interested in it than she was? He wasn't even a student at Canby.

Because the girls of Canby Hall were allowed only incoming calls in their rooms, Andy had stopped to call Matt from the telephone in the reception room of Main Building. As she turned away from the phone, her eyes were caught by the portrait of young Julia Canby that hung high on the wall above Andy's head. In an ornate wooden frame, against a dark background, a tall, slender figure in a maroon Victorian dress and a black cape gazed straight ahead. The dark eyes were solemn, almost sad, the skin pale. Still, there was something in her expression that hinted at . . . what? Andy wasn't sure. A sense of humor? An urge to giggle? Maybe. She imagined a grin playing across the sober mouth. Wasn't there something in the eyes that hinted at a sense of mischief? Repressed, no doubt, considering the times in which she'd lived, but Andy knew it was there, in the eyes and mouth.

Andy leaned against the wall, arms folded

across the front of her blue sleeveless blouse. What sort of mischief would have appealed to a Victorian girl? Putting spiders in people's beds? Sliding down the varnished banisters in those big mansions? Climbing out a second-story window and down the ivy to sneak into town?

Annoyed with herself for becoming interested in the portrait, Andy shook her head and turned to leave. Later she told herself firmly that it was because she'd been so caught up in fantasies about nineteenth-century mischief that the portrait seemed, for just the tiniest second, to deliver a big, deliberate wink in her direction.

Andy jumped and then, embarrassed, glanced quickly around. But she was alone in the reception room. Thank goodness! Andy thought. People would send for the white-coats if they saw her jump because of nothing but a portrait's wink.

A wink? From a painting? She'd been studying too hard. Here I am, she lectured herself with a sheepish grin, teasing Jane about getting lost in that diary when *I'm* seeing a dead person in a painting throwing winks my way. Wouldn't Jane just hoot if she knew?

Shaking her head again, Andy turned and ran out into approaching twilight without giving the portrait another glance.

All three occupants of Room 407 had very different studying styles. Jane retreated to her

Wedgwood blue corner, usually still wearing her pleated skirt and crew-neck sweater. Surrounded by a hodge-podge of books, apple cores, candy wrappers, papers, and soda cans, she could shut out the world and concentrate totally on the task at hand.

Andy needed far less concentration and often played music, listening on headphones, as she worked on her assignments. Rather than messing up her neatly made bed, she usually sat on the floor, legs crossed, leaning against her bed, wearing pajamas and robe. Munching on goodies from the "Care" package mailed from her parents' Chicago restaurant, she tackled her studies in an organized fashion, every now and then humming or tossing off a casual comment to her roommates. Periodically and without warning, she would jump up and do a series of calisthenics, to, as she put it, "get the blood moving again."

Toby had a harder time studying than either of her roommates. Being cooped up inside was always difficult for her. She preferred wide, open spaces, and her little area of the room didn't qualify as either wide or open. The rainbow bedspread she'd purchased during a trip to Boston was cheerful enough, and the tea bag she'd hung from the ceiling over her bed without explanation provided a touch of whimsy. But however cheerful, she found the space confining. Weather permitting during the day, she often studied outside under a tree or on a rock beside the pond. But tonight she lay crosswise on her bed, legs bent up in the air behind her, curly red hair disheveled as she pored over a geometry text-book. Every few minutes, a hefty groan came from her.

"Toby, please!" Andy finally cried. "Will you cease and desist with those grotesque noises! I can hear them even through my head-phones!"

"Sorry." But two minutes later, she did it again and Andy had to toss a banana at her. It slapped against Toby's arm, startling her. But when she saw what it was, she grinned at Andy, picked up the banana, calmly peeled it, and began to eat. Andy grinned back before switching her attention to Jane. Although she had been forced to tear herself away from the library when it closed at nine o'clock, she had copied pages of notes from the diary and was now totally lost in them.

"Jane Barrett!" Andy commanded, clapping her hands to get Jane's attention. "You are supposed to be studying! Why are you wasting time poring over those silly old notes? Which, I might add, you shouldn't have wasted so much time taking in the first place."

"I *beg* your pardon," Jane retorted haught-ily. "I happen to be studying two subjects at the same time, Andrea. I am studying history *and* literature. So the notes I took from Julia

Canby's diary certainly couldn't be called a waste of time."

Andy shook her dark hair. "I don't call a diary history. It's just stuff written by someone a long time ago. It's probably full of recipes for homemade jam and gingerbread and instructions on how to make your own soap."

"Don't be ridiculous! Julie Canby wasn't a pioneer woman. She was gentry!"

Andy looked at Toby. "Gentry?" they echoed in one voice.

"Yes, gentry. My goodness, she lived right here on campus before it was a campus, you know that. That gorgeous brick building P. A. lives in now was her home. The Canbys go back almost as far as *my* family."

"Oh, well, ex-cu-use me," Andy said, getting up and stretching out on her bed. "If she was *that* high society, she certainly didn't make her own soap."

"Of course she didn't." Having made her point, Jane's voice grew calm. "Listen to this. . .

'Papa has instructed Mathilde to have several new dresses made for me. I made her promise to order at least one in royal blue velvet. I can't think where I shall wear the dresses, but it is generous of Papa, nevertheless.' "

"Doesn't sound like she leads a very exciting life," Andy commented. "I wouldn't have any trouble finding places to wear three or four new outfits."

"I know," Jane agreed. "Her father's worse than any of our parents. I went to Europe with my folks two summers ago, and I didn't get to do much on my own, either, so I know how Julia feels."

"Felt," Andy corrected sternly.

"Um-hum. I guess Mathilde must be her governess or companion, something like that. Julia isn't allowed to take a single step without her."

"*Wasn't* allowed," Andy said, unrelenting.

"Um-hum. The poor girl. Doesn't sound like Mathilde has much of a sense of humor, either."

"I don't know," Andy said, shaking her head, "but it all sounds very boring to me. So why are you stuck on those notes as if they held the Secret to True Happiness in Life?"

"It's *not* boring! It's fascinating, reading about a girl just like me who lived a long time ago."

"If she lived a long time ago," Andy pointed out matter-of-factly, "then she's not just like you. Times have changed, Jane, in case you haven't noticed."

"Of course I've noticed. That's just the point. It'll be fascinating to read about the differences between her life and mine."

"I wonder if she was as stubborn as you are," Andy muttered, rolling over onto her back.

"I sure loved that little music box," Toby said dreamily. "We don't have things like that at the ranch. One of the hands would just break them, probably. My mom used to have some little figurines that she kept on the windowsills in the front room, but when she died, my dad put them all away. Maybe I'll look for them when I go home this summer."

Five minutes later, she was sound asleep, with Andy following suit shortly thereafter. Jane stayed awake reading and rereading her notes until her eyelids refused to stay open any longer.

She was almost asleep when she heard the music. Although it sounded far away, Jane recognized the melody. It was the tune from Julia Canby's music box. But it couldn't be. The music box couldn't be checked out of the library, the librarian had said so. Did someone have a record of the song? Even if they did, Jane thought drowsily, why would someone be playing "The Skaters Waltz" in May, when ice on the pond was nothing more than a distant memory? She must be dreaming. Too much time spent on those notes, no doubt.

She was humming the tune when she fell asleep.

CHAPTER FOUR

The following morning, Jane said nothing to Andy or Toby about the music. After all, she'd been half-asleep when she heard it. She had probably imagined it. Hadn't she been thinking about Julia Canby at the time? No wonder that particular tune had slid into her mind. She knew she couldn't really have heard it, because nothing in the exhibit was allowed to leave the library.

Besides, the last thing in the world Andy needed to hear from Jane was that now Jane was hearing things. Andy already thought her roommate was spending too much time with that diary. Jane decided that whether she'd actually heard anything or not, this was something she would keep to herself.

"Anybody got plans for this gorgeous Sunday?" she asked lightly as she slipped into khaki pleated shorts and a matching camp shirt. Toby and Andy were already dressed and anxious to get to the dining hall for breakfast.

Andy nodded. "I'm going to call Matt and blackmail him into coming over to study with me today. I've hardly seen him at all since last weekend." She grinned. "I'll tell him that if he doesn't join me, I'll spread it all over Oakley's campus that he only has to shave twice a week. That'll get him over here faster than I can say 'Gillette.'"

Jane clipped her hair back on each side of her oval face with a gold barrette. "What about you, Toby? Want to go to the library with me?"

Toby nodded, but Andy said in a warning tone, "Jane, you aren't going to bury yourself in that diary again, are you? What about finals? You need to study."

Jane's back went stiff. Dropping her silver-backed hairbrush on her dresser, she said coolly, "I *am* going to be studying. Isn't that what most people go to the library to do? But studying isn't going to take up my whole Sunday."

"Well, it should," Andy retorted grumpily as the three of them left the room. She couldn't understand what Jane saw in that old diary. What difference did it make what had happened to Julia Canby so many years ago? Everything had been different then. So why bother reading it? What a waste of time! Maybe, she thought as they entered the dining hall, there would be a huge crowd at the exhibit today, and Jane wouldn't be able to get within a foot of that useless diary. Then she could study English literature and ensure that she'd walk off with that award, hands down.

They were waiting in line, trays in hand, when their next-door neighbors, Dee and Maggie, walked up. "Hey!" blonde Californian Dee asked, "you guys hear any weird music last night after Lights Out?" Short, curly-haired Maggie said, "It wasn't weird, Dee. It was 'The Skaters Waltz.' Smiling at Jane and her roommates, she said tolerantly, "Dee doesn't understand music you can't surf to. And as far as I know, there *isn't* any 'Surfers Waltz.'"

Dee gave her a playful smack on the arm. "Well, what about it, guys? Were we hearing things, or what?"

Jane hesitated. She hadn't mentioned hearing the music box melody because she wasn't really sure she had heard it. But if Dee and Maggie had. . .

Before she could say anything, Penny Vanderark, who had just joined them and heard that last part of their conversation, said, "I heard it. I figured either I was dreaming or you guys were doing some strange musical experiment, because it sure didn't sound like your usual stuff."

Toby frowned and said, "*I* didn't hear anything," as if that surprised her.

Everyone laughed. "Of course you didn't, Toby," Andy said. "You sleep as if you've just been given major anesthesia. You wouldn't hear a parade if a marching band made your bed part of the parade route."

Toby joined in the laughter, the line moved ahead, and nothing more was said about the music. But Jane felt very relieved to find that she hadn't been hearing things. Of course she'd known all along that she hadn't been imagining things. As an aspiring writer she liked to invent stories, but she had never yet invented sounds!

Later, as Jane entered the cool, shadowed library, she wondered again just exactly where that music *had* come from. The music box was sitting securely on the velvet square, just where it was supposed to be. Shrugging, Jane went straight to the diary to begin taking notes before people arrived to view the exhibit. Toby followed close behind, anxious for more time with the music box.

"Honestly!" Andy told Matt in exasperation, "I just don't see the magic in that old exhibit. And Jane and Toby couldn't wait to get back to the library. Toby, of all people! She can't stand to be inside for more than twenty minutes at a time and there she was, headed for the library!" She stared at Matt with wide eyes. "On purpose! All because of some old music box." She shook her head. "I just don't get it."

They were sitting on an old Army blanket of Matt's, under one of the big old trees on campus. Dotted all across the sweeping expanse of green lawn were other blankets occupied by other students intent on killing two birds with one stone: studying for finals while basking in the sun.

"Andy," Matt said, leaning against the trunk of their tree, "you're the most 'now' person I've ever met. You don't get nervous worrying about what might happen tomorrow, the way lots of people do, and you don't look backward, either. And that's great. It's one of the things I like most about you. But. . ."

Uh-oh, Andy thought, here it comes! Matt had a strong sense of logic. His calm, rational approach to life sometimes clashed with her sense of the dramatic. Although they shared an interest in theater and dance, Matt's role was a technical one: he had designed and managed the lighting for several performances at Oakley and Canby, including a dance recital featuring Andy. Sometimes he just didn't understand Andy's more emotional reaction to things.

"But maybe Jane and Toby have a stronger sense of history than you do," he finished calmly.

Andy groaned silently. There he went, being rational again. Of *course* Jane and Toby were more interested in the past than she was. Almost anyone was. But tall, sweet, handsome Matt wasn't supposed to point that out. He was supposed to understand *her* point of view.

Swallowing her irritation, she changed the subject. She told him about the Literature Award. "And," she finished, "Jane will probably have to write an essay before the final decision is made. And where is she going to find the time if she's spending every waking moment buried in that musty old book?" Then she realized she hadn't changed the subject at all. Like a boomerang she was right back where she'd started.

"She'll find the time," Matt assured her. "You know Jane. She may have trouble getting started sometimes, but she always gets the job done."

Andy nodded reluctantly. She knew Matt was right. Shaking her head, she said, "Okay, okay. I'll quit nagging her about her travels into the dusty past. *If* she makes time to study for finals." Her voice became more cheerful. "We can't have any dummies in Baker Hall. It's just not allowed!"

Matt laughed and stretched out on the blanket, a thick book in his hands. "Well, speaking of dummies *and* the past, if I don't study one right now, I'm going to become the other.

How about us doing some heavy mental exercise?"

Another groan, but again Andy knew he was right. If she herself didn't hit the books, how could she complain about anyone else ignoring her studies? Flopping down beside Matt, she opened her notebook.

In the library, Jane *was* ignoring her studies. Toby had spent an entranced fifteen minutes with the music box and then opted for the out-of-doors, leaving Jane behind. Now, sole occupant of the cool, dim corner where she sat hunched over the little leather diary, Jane was once again lost in Julia Canby's long-ago life.

February 8, 1897
Dear Diary,
   Papa let Mathilde take me ice-skating today. The sun was shining and it was a lovely day, but Mathilde grumbled the whole time. She doesn't seem to know the first thing about having fun. There were so many people my age on the pond. I wasn't allowed to talk to any of them. They looked like they were having a splendid time. I wanted so much to join them. But Papa says I must be formally introduced before I can talk to anyone. But I don't see how that's possible, when

there is no one to introduce me. How can
I get to know people if I cannot talk to
them?

I miss Clarice so!"

The last sentence in the entry piqued Jane's
curiosity. Since there were now a few students
gathered around the glass case, which made
her feel guilty about monopolizing the diary,
she decided to exchange it for one of the letters
written to Julia. She wondered if they were
from the "Clarice" mentioned in the diary.

The one she selected from the pile was
indeed from Clarice. And it did tell Jane
something about young Julia.

Dear Julia,

I miss you so much! When are you
coming home? I don't have anyone to giggle with late at night. That silly simp
Livonia DeVoe was our overnight guest
on Wednesday, but she's no fun. Mama
invited her. All Vonnie talks about are
those dumb horses of hers. Everyone asks
me about you. They want to know why
your father is keeping you over there.

That nice John Ludlow (remember,
the one you thought was so handsome?)
called here twice last week. Papa thought
he was here to see me and teased me about
it. But he was here asking about you.

He looks so forlorn. Can't you talk your father into bringing you back here where you belong?

> Your best friend,
> Clarice Van der Horn

Jane let the tissue-thin piece of stationery fall into her lap. So. Julia Canby had had a sense of humor. She had been popular. Not only that, at thirteen, boys were already attracted to her. The portrait in Main Building probably didn't do her justice.

So how could her father expect her to live such an isolated, lonely life in Europe? Why didn't he see to it that she had friends? Grown-ups could be so dense sometimes, and apparently that had been true even in Victorian times.

A glance up at the clock made Jane realize guiltily that the day was nearly over, and she hadn't so much as touched a textbook. She could almost hear Andy admonishing, "Jane! Get your nose out of that musty old letter, and get to work on the here and now!"

Laughing softly to herself, Jane got up and returned the letter to its proper place. She picked up her books and went out into the fading sunshine, her mind still on Julia Canby and the friends who had missed her so much.

Later, Jane told herself that that was why it happened. Her preoccupation with the diary had to be the reason she thought she saw what she saw.

Because what she thought she saw as she came around a corner and began walking toward the pond was . . . Julia Canby.

Jane stopped in her tracks, her mouth a round *O* of surprise. Dressed in the maroon, floor-length dress and the black cloak seen in the portrait, dark curls cascading down her back, the girl who looked like Julia Canby slipped into a grove of trees and disappeared.

"I was seeing things," a very pale Jane whispered to herself as she sank, weak-kneed, onto a large boulder. That's all, I was just seeing things. Andy's right — I've been spending far too much time with that diary, she thought. It's time to put it aside and turn to books that don't stimulate the imagination. Books like Canby Hall's government and Latin and literature textbooks. Boring, boring, boring. But safe, safe, safe!

She could just imagine Andy's reaction if she ran back to the room and said, Guess who I just ran into down by the pond! Jane laughed aloud, startling herself and a bluejay sitting on a neighboring rock. After giving her a look that clearly said, "All humans are mentally unbalanced," the bird flew away. Jane decided that a departure wasn't such a bad idea. She was sure she couldn't handle another apparition so soon. She got up and hurried away, too.

CHAPTER FIVE

In spite of her resolution earlier that day, Jane spent most of the evening sitting on her bed lost in silent thought. Had she or hadn't she seen something down by the pond? And if she *had* seen something, what was it? Okay, so it had looked like the girl in the portrait. Big deal. That was so ridiculous it wasn't even worth thinking about. I, she told herself firmly, am an educated, intelligent, rational, nineteen-eighties person. I do *not* believe in ghosts, spirits of any sort, apparitions, or supernatural beings who wander around the earth looking for humans to annoy. So whatever I saw was of this earth. Now all I have to do is figure out *what* it was, and why it looked so much like Julia Canby.

Andy was worried about Jane. They were all supposed to be studying, but there Jane sat, staring straight ahead and fidgeting nervously with the fringe on her bedspread. Jane never fidgeted. And she hadn't opened a single book or picked up a pen. And she hadn't said a word at dinner. What was the matter with her? If this was what happened to people who spent too much time in a library, Andy was glad she'd done her studying out in the fresh air.

"Jane. Jane!"

"Hmmm?"

"What's with you? You're supposed to be studying. Where *are* you anyway?"

Jane shook her head. "I'm . . . I'm just thinking, that's all." She was not about to tell anyone, least of all Andy, what she'd seen or thought she'd seen.

"Well, you're not supposed to be thinking. You're supposed to be studying. Has Merrie said anything to you about you and Penny and Gigi having to write an essay? To decide who gets the Lit Award?"

Jane shook her head no, but Toby lifted her head just then. "Dee and Maggie told me there *will* be an essay contest. They said Merrie told them this afternoon."

Jane came out of her fog with a groan. "Oh, great! When am I going to find the time to write an essay? I already feel like someone is stealing huge chunks of time from my day and hiding them."

"Yeah," Andy said sarcastically, her eyes focusing on the unopened textbooks cluttering Jane's bed, "I can see how overburdened you are. Staring straight ahead is hard work. You must be exhausted."

Jane hated sarcasm. Her anger at Andy brought her back to reality. She'd been imaging things today, and that was that, period! She had things to do, and there wasn't a whole lot of time left between now and finals. She'd better get to work.

"I have an idea," she said slowly as she opened her Latin book. "Toby, did Dee or Maggie say what the essays have to be about?"

"Your choice," Toby answered without looking up. "You get to pick the topic."

Jane's eyes lit up. "No kidding? We don't have to dissect one of the classics or do a biography of a Russian writer?"

Toby shook her head. "Nope. Not according to Dee. Ms. Allardyce already knows you three know your stuff in literature. I guess she just wants to see who learned the most about writing from your lit classes. So you can pick any topic you want. That's what Dee said, anyway."

"What do you have in mind, Jane?" Andy wanted to know. "I can practically see the wheels turning from here."

"The diary," Jane said excitedly, "it's perfect! I can write an essay on Julia Canby and how her life was different from ours. And I can put some of Canby's history into my paper. How it got started, that kind of stuff."

Andy covered her face with her hands.

"Jane," she mumbled through her fingers, "I do *not* want to hear one more word about that diary! Can't you pick some other topic? If you're going to be writing about that book, you'll be buried in it every second from now on." She lifted her head and glared at Jane. "Why can't you write about 'Why People Slurp Their Food at the Table,' or 'Do Blondes Have More Fun?' or 'The Most Fun I Ever Had at the Dentist'? Nice, normal subjects like that?"

Toby laughed. Jane didn't. She was already delving into her notes from Julia's diary, studying them with fierce concentration.

And when Jane Barrett made up her mind, there was no changing it. Now she had obviously made up her mind about using the diary for her essay. "You just want an excuse to spend more time reading that dumb little book," Andy grumbled. Jane gave no sign that she'd heard. Andy shrugged and returned to her own studies.

That night, it was Andy who heard the music box melody. Jane had fallen asleep over her notes and Toby had done the same minutes later. Annoyed with Jane's attitude, Andy was restless. She was lying on her back, legs crossed in the air, wondering if Jane's idea about the essay could possibly be a stroke of genius, when the unmistakable strains of "The Skaters Waltz" sounded faintly in the dark.

Andy sat up. Maggie and Dee had said it

wasn't their music. Then whose was it? Why
hadn't she ever heard it before? Except at the
ice pond. She'd heard it there. But that had
been in the dead of winter. This was May and
there was no ice on the pond. Besides, that
recording had been of an orchestra. This
sound was not only the tune itself, it was
exactly the same tinkling sound as that of the
music box. The very same music box that was
not supposed to leave the library. If someone
had sneaked it out, against the rules, they
wouldn't be foolish enough to only play it
late at night, would they? When there were
no other noises to hide the sound? No, this
seemed much more like a deliberate attempt
to *make* the melody be heard. And why would
anyone do that?

Unable to figure it out, Andy finally fell
asleep.

The next day, she had an idea. "I'm going
to call Cary," she told Toby as they walked
to their first class. Jane had risen late, as usual,
and was still getting dressed. "He hasn't seen
much of Jane since the exhibit arrived. I'll bet
he's not exactly thrilled about that. Maybe he
can think of something to get her out of that
library. After all, she must be missing him,
too!"

Cary Slade was lead guitarist for Oakley
Prep's rock band, Ambulance. Although his
longish blond hair and single earring con-

trasted sharply with Jane's traditional good looks, they shared the same background. But while Jane embraced the upper-class values instilled in her, Cary rebelled against his. His music, his manner of dress, and his attitude about wealth and propriety, were all expressions of his disdain for his social position. But Jane and Cary had worked out most of their differences. Although they argued occasionally about what Cary called the unfairness of unearned wealth, for the most part they accepted their opposing viewpoints. As Cary liked to point out, Jane had been attracted to him originally because he was "different" and "interesting." Had he been exactly like her, she probably would have become bored with the relationship very quickly.

"Cary will help," Andy told Toby. "He'll get Jane's nose out of that book. Maybe he can talk her into writing her essay on rock groups instead of Julia Canby. I'll call him during lunch hour."

But to Andy's dismay, Cary refused to help. He didn't share her concern about the time Jane was spending with the diary. "I think it's great that Jane's interested in something out of the ordinary," he said when Andy had explained the situation. "She's expanding her horizons."

"She's expanding herself right into the *past*," Andy argued. "That's going backward!

How can that do her any good?" She was disappointed by Cary's reaction. She had been so sure he would help.

Instead Cary sighed audibly and said, "Andy, Andy, Andy. For a bright girl, your vision is just a bit narrow. Me, I think it's great that Jane is taking an interest in this. And if I do talk to her, I'll tell her exactly that."

"Okay, okay," Andy said, giving in. She knew when she was licked. "But can we at least plan a study day — maybe Saturday — when we can all get together at Canby and cram for finals? That's the only way I can think of to make sure Jane at least opens some books other than that diary."

"Sounds good. Sure. And tell Jane to call me later, okay?"

"Well, I'll tell her," Andy agreed doubtfully, "but I don't think you've been listening to me. She's only got one thing on her mind, and it's *not* someone as current as you. See you Saturday." And she hung up, thinking that maybe, just maybe, she'd planted a tiny seed of worry in Cary's mind with that last remark. Maybe after he'd thought about what she'd said, he'd change his mind and come running to yank Jane out of the past. Maybe.

Outside, she hurried with long strides toward her English class. Although the day was as beautiful as the one before it, her mood was sour. She missed Matt and knew that she wouldn't see much more of him until finals were behind them. And she was extremely annoyed with both Jane and Cary. It was bad enough that Jane was delving into the past with gusto. Now she had Cary supporting her!

So, when a tall, slender figure dressed in Victorian clothing drifted out from behind Main Building some distance from Andy, her response was anger, not shock or fear.

"Oh, stop it!" she yelled, "that's not funny!" The figure hesitated, glancing over in Andy's direction through a cloud of long, dark, wavy hair.

Andy moved closer, but as she did, the figure began backing away. "Where did you get those clothes? And that wig?" Andy shouted. The sun was in her eyes and it was difficult to see clearly. But she was sure she knew who the clothes and wig were hiding. It had to be Gigi Norton. This was just the sort of stunt she would pull. She was probably jealous of all the attention the Julia Canby exhibit was getting and had chosen this ghostly impersonation to distract everyone. What a silly, childish prank! If Jane saw this she would become very upset. And the last thing Andy needed right now was an upset Jane.

Shielding her eyes from the sun, she shouted, "Gigi, this is really dumb! It's the dumbest thing you've ever done! You're not fooling anyone!"

The figure in the maroon dress and black cape stood stock-still for just another moment. Then it laughed lightly and vanished.

Andy shook her head in disgust. She hoped no one else had seen what she'd seen. With all of the fuss being made over Julia right now, some girls on campus could get really rattled by a sight like that.

Anxious to get to Gigi and put an end to her mischief, Andy turned a corner.

And ran smack into Gigi Norton, who was wearing a white skirt and a red and white striped top, *not* a maroon dress and black cloak. There was no bundle of hastily discarded Victorian clothing anywhere in sight. And her dark hair lay flat and lifeless as always, with no sign that it had, only moments earlier, been mussed by the removal of a wig. The expression on her face was one of annoyance, not guilt or excitement.

Andy stared at her in disbelief.

CHAPTER SIX

Andy continued to stare. "Where did *you* come from?" she burst out.

Gigi leered at her. "Where do you think, dummy? Didn't you ever take biology?"

"No, I mean where did you come from just now?"

"Dining hall. Not that it's any of your business. What's the matter with you, anyway? You look like you just saw a ghost."

A high-pitched giggle escaped Andy's lips. Then she quickly regained control. "Don't be silly! I just wasn't expecting anyone to be skulking around, that's all."

"I wasn't skulking any more than you were! This is my campus, too, Cord, even if you and your pals like to pretend you own it."

Suddenly unable to think of any reason why she was talking to this unpleasant person, Andy whirled away without another word. Why had she bothered to get out of bed that morning? She'd had better days when she was sick and miserable! Honestly!

Concentrating in English class wasn't easy. Andy'd been wrong about Gigi masquerading as Julia Canby, and that unsettled her. There hadn't been anyone else in the area, and she'd run into Gigi immediately after seeing the figure in Victorian clothes. Gigi couldn't possibly have changed clothes. There hadn't been enough time.

But if it hadn't been Gigi . . . then who? Was it possible that she really hadn't seen anything at all? That she'd simply had her mind on Julia Canby so much that her eyes had played tricks on her?

No, Andy told herself firmly as she opened her English book, I am not the sort of person who sees things. I saw what I saw! Elbow resting on the desk, chin propped on a cupped hand, she stared out the window. The question was, was she sure enough of what she'd seen to tell anyone else? Jane? Certainly not! Jane was already too involved in all of this Julia Canby stuff. Toby? Maybe. Sometimes Toby had a unique way of looking at things. Maybe she'd have a logical explanation for what Andy had seen.

The minute classes were over for the day, Andy went looking for Toby. She found her roommate sitting on a rock beside the pond, her nose in a book. But before Andy could say anything, Toby looked up and said, "I thought if I sat here long enough, maybe I'd see her."

"See who?" Andy took a seat on a companion rock.

"The ghost."

Andy's jaw dropped. "What ghost?"

"Julia Canby's ghost," Toby answered calmly, brushing one red wave away from her cheek. "Tina Loftis saw her today, right here on this very spot."

Andy tried a laugh, and to her surprise, it worked. "What *are* you talking about?" There, her voice wasn't at all shaky.

"I passed Tina on my way to geometry class. She was running and her face was the color of old hay. She said she'd just seen Julia Canby right here at the pond."

"That's crazy." Wasn't it?

Toby shrugged. "I asked her if she was sure that's what she'd seen. She shouted at me that she'd looked at that portrait of Julia every day for the past two years. She said she'd know her anywhere."

There was silence for a moment. Then Andy tried another laugh. This one didn't work as well. It came out sounding more like she was choking than laughing. "She'd know her anywhere? Isn't that just the silliest thing you've ever heard?"

But Toby wasn't laughing. She just sat on

her rock, looking at Andy with wide eyes. "Why is it silly? Wouldn't *you* know Julia Canby if you saw her?"

Yes, I certainly would, Andy thought, picturing for a moment the figure in Victorian clothing she'd seen earlier. "Oh, Toby! I don't *expect* to see her. Someone dressed like her, maybe. But not *her*. That's impossible."

To her astonishment, Toby shook her head. "Oh, I don't know," she said doubtfully. "Tina seemed awfully positive."

"To-by! Get real! There *is* no Julia Canby."

"Well, there was once." Toby's voice sounded maddeningly calm.

"But she wouldn't go running around all over the place where people could *see* her *now*," Andy said.

"Maybe she's looking for something," Toby said, laughing. She stood up. "But it's getting late and I've got stuff to do. I guess if Julia Canby wanted me to see her, she'd have shown up by now." And taking one last glance around, she turned to leave.

"Toby," Andy said quickly, "I don't think we should mention any of this to Jane." She got up and walked over to Toby. "The last thing in the world she needs to hear right now is this silly story of Tina's. She's already having trouble concentrating on anything but that diary and those letters. So can we just keep this to ourselves?"

Again, Toby looked doubtful. "I don't think Tina's going to keep this to herself. My goodness, she was practically shouting the whole story when she told me about it. It's probably all over campus now."

Andy grimaced. "I hope you're wrong about that. It wouldn't be good for anyone." But as they headed for Baker House, Andy had a feeling Toby was right.

She was. All of Baker House was buzzing with the story of Julia Canby's ghost when Andy and Toby arrived. Happy to be distracted from the anxiety of approaching finals, everyone had latched onto Tina's story. Small clusters of girls crowded the lower hall, chattering with excitement.

Dee and Maggie came running up to Andy and Toby. "Hi!" Maggie cried, clutching Andy's arm. "Have you heard? It's all over school. Julia Canby is here! Right here at Canby Hall!"

Before Andy or Toby could comment, Dee added, "The story is, she's angry because her privacy's been invaded."

"So she's come back to get her things," Maggie finished quickly.

Andy's annoyed laugh rang through the corridor. "Cut it out, you two!" she scolded sharply, moving through the crowd as she spoke. "Everyone is being totally ridiculous! The only place you're going to see Julia Canby on this campus is in an oil painting at

Main Building." Stopping suddenly, she turned to a flustered Maggie to demand, "Does Jane know about all this silliness?"

Maggie nodded. Then she thrust out her chin in defiance. "And *she* believes it!"

Andy groaned. "Of course she does!" They hurried toward Room 407. "This is exactly what Jane's been waiting for. Now everyone on campus is as interested in the antique Miss Canby as Jane is. If I didn't know Jane better, I'd think it was *her* parading around campus dressed in old clothing." She reached for the doorknob to their room. "Now we'll never get her away from that stuff of Julia's. She's probably wallowing in it right this minute."

Whether or not wallowing was the right word, Jane was, indeed, immersed in her notes from Julia's diary when Andy and her companions entered the room. Andy flopped down on her bed, facing Jane. "See?" she said to the others, "what did I tell you? Our roomie here has taken another time-travel trip into the distant past. And she's happy about it. Look at the goofy expression on her face."

As Toby sat down on her own bed and invited Dee and Maggie to do the same, Jane smiled a greeting at all of them. "I guess you've heard," she said softly. "Now I can tell you something that's been driving me crazy. I didn't tell you before because I was afraid you'd send the people in white coats after me."

She laughed self-consciously. "And I'd get claustrophobic in a padded cell."

Andy lifted her head. "Don't tell me, let me guess. Like Mr. Scrooge in *A Christmas Carol*, you, too, have been visited by vestiges of the past."

Jane smiled again. "How did you know? I didn't tell anyone. You're so smart, Andy."

Andy frowned at the compliment. It was easy enough to dismiss Tina's story about seeing Julia Canby. Tina was the sort of person who read only science-fiction and talked constantly about aliens from other planets. But Jane . . . well, Jane was ordinarily as level-headed as they came. Jane didn't make up crazy stories just to get attention. There was probably something in the Barrett genes that prevented that sort of thing.

"Are you telling us you saw her, too?" Toby asked Jane. "The ghost, I mean?"

"That's exactly what I'm telling you. Yesterday. Down by the pond. I . . . I thought it was just my imagination, because I'd been spending so much time with Julia's diary. And even if it wasn't my imagination, I knew you'd think it was."

"You can say that again," Andy said darkly.

Ignoring her, Jane continued. "I'm not kidding, the person I saw looked exactly like Julia Canby! It was bizarre!"

Andy knew she should admit that she, too, had seen something. But how could she, when she wasn't at all sure exactly what she'd seen? Besides, wouldn't encouraging Jane now be the worst thing she could do?

"Bizarre is the right word," she said, lying back against her bed pillows. "It's bizarre that one of the smartest girls in this school, meaning you, Jane, is falling for someone's silly joke."

A look of hurt spread across Jane's face. "It doesn't have anything to do with being smart," she said, her tone defensive. "I just know what I saw, that's all. And Tina saw it, too. So I know I wasn't seeing things. What does that have to do with being smart?"

"There *are* no ghosts," Andy said firmly. "Not here, not anywhere. And we all know that. I can't believe we're even having this conversation."

"Oh, I don't know," Jane said, keeping her voice deliberately casual. "There's old Oliver Barrett. My whole family knows about him. And my family isn't exactly stupid, Andy."

"Who's Oliver Barrett?"

Jane leaned forward, her eyes sparkling. "My great-great-grandfather. Every once in a while, according to my family, he pops up at the old mansion, checking up on us to see if we're behaving properly." She laughed lightly. "I never asked what he'd do to someone who *wasn't* behaving properly, since I was pretty sure that would be me. I really didn't want to know what old Ollie would do to me."

"Gosh," a wide-eyed Maggie wanted to know, "how did you know he was there?"

Jane shrugged. "Oh, you know: doors opening and shutting all by themselves, stairs creaking, lights dimming, that kind of stuff. The telephone would ring, and there wouldn't be anyone on the line."

"Jane," Andy said flatly, "your great-great-grandfather wouldn't know the first thing about how to use a telephone."

Jane giggled. "That's probably why there was never anyone on the line when we answered. Old Ollie just couldn't get the hang of a new-fangled contraption like the telephone."

"Very funny." But Andy didn't look amused. "Toby, tell these people they've all gone totally bananas."

But Toby did no such thing. "Back home," she said softly, gazing up at the tea bag hanging over her bed, "there's Old Jake."

"Who's he?" Dee asked. Andy hid her head in her hands, sensing what was coming.

"An old miner," Toby replied. "He'd been prospecting a big piece of land in the desert for years, hunting for silver. But, so the story goes, he forgot to stake a legitimate claim on it. And after a while, some men came and took the mine away from him. There wasn't anything he could do to stop them, since he didn't have any papers for the mine. They had guns and chased him away. He died alone, broke, and real angry at the whole world. Now everyone says he haunts the mine. It's deserted, has been for a long time, but people have seen his miner's light late at night. Kids in the area say they've talked to him when they were playing near the mine. And some of the ranchers say they've had supplies stolen by a bent little old man in overalls and a dirty, wide-brimmed hat."

Andy threw her hands up in the air. "I give up!" she cried. "Studying for finals has done it. You've all gone over the edge, smack into the Twilight Zone."

Jane tipped her head, a grin playing around her lips. "Are you sure there are no ghosts, Andy? Are you absolutely, positively positive?"

For once in her life, Andy had no answer.

CHAPTER SEVEN

The dining hall was in chaos that night, with only one topic of conversation: Julia Canby's "presence" on campus. Some girls, like Andy, thought the sightings utter nonsense and said so. Others found the whole business hysterically funny and joked about it. The group Jane gravitated toward, however, took it seriously and discussed it in the same way. Each girl had a ghost story of her own to tell and Jane listened attentively, ignoring Andy's increasing irritation.

After the third story (an aunt who had lived in someone's attic for one hundred and twenty-two years), Andy jumped to her feet. "You are all being ridiculous!" she cried in exasperation. "Julia Canby is *not* on this campus!" She picked up her tray, her dinner only half-eaten. "And if she planned to pay us a visit, do you honestly think she'd pick a day when we're having creamed chipped beef on toast?" With that, she turned on her heels, calling over her shoulder to Jane, "I'm going to see if Maggie wants to go over to Oakley in search of some sanity. See you crazy people later."

Jane didn't seem the least bit upset by Andy's departure. What she considered Andy's closed mind merely annoyed her. She wondered what Cary would think of all the stories. Resolving to call him after dinner, she turned her attention to yet another story, this one about a grandmother who reportedly made regular appearances during the Christmas holidays.

At Oakley after agreeing to meet Maggie back at the Oakley library to walk home, Andy found Matt sitting on a sofa in the student lounge. He was deep in study, an opened book on his lap. Slightly out of breath from her walk, she flopped down beside him. "You wouldn't believe what's going on over there!" she said, waving a hand toward Canby. "Half the school has flipped out. They're all seeing things!"

Matt lifted his head. He knew Andy very well and, for the most part, he loved her unbridled enthusiasm for life. But there were those times, like now, when something knocked her off-balance. He dreaded those times because he hadn't yet figured out how to restore her equilibrium. The only thing he *had* figured out was that usually she had to find her own way back out of her emotional somersaults.

"So what's going on?" he asked, settling an arm around her shoulders.

Sighing, she told him, punctuating her story with arm gestures, as if she were refereeing a football game. When she had finished, she looked at Matt expectantly. "So," she asked when he remained silent, "what do I do?"

This was the part he hated. No matter what he came up with, it wouldn't be the answer she was looking for. The best idea was to just be supportive. "You'll think of something," he said firmly, knowing that that was not only the safest answer, it was the most accurate one.

She studied her sandal-clad feet. "Well, I don't see *how*." She'd told him about seeing the figure down by the pond. What she hadn't told him was how that sighting, coupled with the rumors at school, had sent her normal thinking processes into a tailspin. She was beginning to feel as if she'd been on a merry-go-round too long. She *had* seen Julia Canby, she *hadn't* seen Julia Canby, everyone at school was crazy, no, *she* was the one who was crazy . . . it was maddening. It was all so silly. And yet there *were* people who were taking it seriously. She wasn't becoming one of them, was she?

Shaking her head to dismiss such weird

thoughts, she said lightly, "I guess you're right. I'll think of something." Because she didn't want to discuss it anymore.

But they both heard the lack of conviction in her voice. Sighing, she leaned against him. "So," she said, taking the book from his hands, "let me quiz you on your Latin. It'll make me feel useful and I won't feel as guilty about interrupting your studying. Fair enough?"

"Fair enough." They settled back, content to leave the ghost of Julia Canby to others for the moment.

In the cool, well-lighted interior of the Canby Hall library, Jane was comfortably settled in her favorite corner, the leather diary in hand. She'd had a few bad moments earlier, when it seemed that her chances of getting the little book again were about as likely as the chances of Andrea Cord ever attending a seance. Rumors about Julia Canby's presence on campus had created an instant demand for the items on exhibit. When Jane saw the crowd gathered around the glass case, she moaned and turned in dismay toward Toby, who was studying at the table.

"I'll never get near it!" she wailed. "And I've hardly made a dent in it!"

"Yes, you will," Toby said calmly. She nodded toward the group. "Most of those girls are on the Yearbook committee. They have a meeting in the gym in fifteen minutes. I heard someone say so at dinner."

Jane breathed a sigh of relief and waited her turn. When it came, she clutched the diary happily while Toby settled down with several of Julia Canby's letters, the music box open and playing on a little table by her elbow.

February 9, 1897
Dear Diary,

It has been raining all day. In Massachusetts, it would be snowing: light, feathery flakes of white. And in the afternoon, Clarice and I would go sleigh-riding on the hill beside the house. Everyone would come: Jeffrey and Melinda and Robert and Sara, and afterwards we would go up to the house and have cocoa and biscuits. Maybe that nice John Ludlow would come, too.

A rainy afternoon in London isn't nearly so much fun. If only Clarice could have come with me. At least I'd have somebody to talk to. I don't know how Papa expects me to make friends. I never meet anyone my own age. Everyone I've been introduced to through relatives has been old and boring and that's the truth, Diary.

And I'm homesick.

Jane let the diary fall into her lap. Julia sounded so lonely. Why couldn't her relatives have seen to it that she was introduced to some Londoners her own age? Sometimes adults could be so thoughtless! At least, she thought gratefully, when we were in Europe Mother and Father saw to it that I had people my own age around.

Glancing around, Jane realized that Toby had left. Her chair was empty, the music box and letters back in the display case. Jane smiled. Ten minutes indoors on a beautiful spring evening was Toby's limit. That was okay with Jane. She liked being alone with the diary. She felt comfortable entering Julia Canby's world all by herself.

She picked up the open book again.

February 10, 1897
Dear Diary,

Guess what? You'll never guess! I met someone today. A young man. Papa doesn't know yet, and I can't imagine how I shall tell him. But I must, because my new friend, Master Edward Lynch, has said he wants to call on me. He is so nice, Diary, so kind, and so very handsome! He is tall and strong, with dark hair and lovely brown eyes. I met him at the livery when our carriage began misbehaving today and we had to exchange it for another. He was waiting with his uncle for their own carriage. When he spoke to me, Diary, I thought I was dreaming. Then, when I was sure I wasn't dreaming, I was so frightened that Mathilde would overhear us and be scandalized that I whispered every word. I was afraid she would have him hung or shot if she caught me talking to him. But she was busy giving instructions to the footman. I was able to talk to Master Lynch for a whole two minutes, long enough to give him our address here at the hotel. And he promised to call on us. Oh, Diary, do you really think he might? He is older than I, probably at least sixteen, and seems quite sophisticated. He was elegantly dressed and very well mannered. What can he see in me? Papa says I'm like a newborn colt, so awkward are my movements. And I'm sure he's right.

Oh, Diary, I so hope Master Lynch calls on us. It would be so lovely to have someone besides Mathilde to talk to.

I must sleep now, if that is possible when I'm so excited. But I've been feeling unusually tired these past few days and rest is necessary.

P. S. He has such a lovely smile!

"*There* you are!" Andy's voice from behind Jane made her jump. "I might have known you'd be hiding in here. C'mon, put that musty old book away. Cary's outside. I brought him back from Oakley with me."

Jane, still lost in 1897 London, looked up. "What? Cary? Here?"

"Very good, Jane, you're catching on quickly. Now try a sentence of two or more words, such as, "I'm coming, Andy.""

Jane couldn't help laughing. "Okay, okay." She closed the book with reluctance, anxious to learn more about Julia's budding romance, if that was what it was, with young Edward Lynch. But Andy was probably doing her a favor. She hadn't had much time for her own romance lately. And patience wasn't really one of Cary Slade's primary virtues.

He was sitting on one of the stone lions flanking the library entrance. Jane smiled as she approached. Cary was one of the best-looking boys she'd ever seen. As far as she was concerned, the single earring and longer-than-average blondish hair only added to his good looks. Lean and rangy in jeans and a gray sleeveless sweatshirt, he aimed a crooked grin in her direction.

"I hear you've been hob-nobbing with the spirit world," he said lazily.

Jane shot Andy an annoyed glance. "Some-one," she said coolly, "has a very big mouth."

Andy laughed and pretended to hide be-hind Matt.

"Don't worry about it," Cary said, sliding off the lion and walking over to Jane. "I've met folks a lot stranger than you. Liked every one of them, too." Linking an arm in hers, he suggested they all go to Main Building because the lobby there held vending machines. "Listen," he said as they walked, "what about this business of studying together on Saturday? That okay with you?"

Jane hesitated. Andy had mentioned Saturday to her, but it had seemed far away at the time, so Jane hadn't really thought about it. She had planned to spend Saturday going over the diary and the letters. But if she said so now, Andy would have a fit and Cary would be hurt. They'd seen so little of each other lately. And she should study, something she hadn't been doing much of since the exhibit arrived. "Sure," she said lightly, wondering if she could photocopy some of the diary's pages to read in her room. "It'll be fun."

"Fun? Studying?" Cary grinned down at her. "Maybe Andy's right. Maybe you have flipped out."

"I just meant it'll be nice for all of us to get together. It's been a while. . . ."

"Right. Now tell me all about your ectoplasmic friend, the now-you-see-her, now-you-don't Miss Julia Canby."

Checking first to make sure Andy wasn't within hearing distance, she filled Cary in on the most recent developments, finishing with, "But Andy is not at all happy about any of this, so let's not talk about it tonight, okay? I can't deal with her when she's upset."

Andy and Matt were laughing as they joined Jane and Cary on the steps of Main Building. "I'm starving!" Andy cried. "I hope they've put fresh goodies in the vending machines. When I was here the other day, the brownies looked like petrified rock." Something tugged at her memory, and she shivered, but she was too intent on the vending machines to concentrate on what had caused the shiver. Matt handed her a fistful of quarters, and she focused her attention on the machine filled with plastic bags and tiny little boxes and packages of cookies until she had what she wanted. Then she led the others into the lobby, planning to find a comfortable place to sit while they enjoyed their snacks.

She was just about to enter the big room when she glanced up and saw the portrait of Julia Canby and remembered why she had shivered earlier. The wink . . . the Victorian girl stared out at her as if to say, "Go ahead. Come on in. I dare you."

"Oh, no," Andy groaned, surprising her companions, "I forgot!" Spinning around, she grabbed Matt's arm. "I cannot sit in a room with a portrait of Julia Canby. Not tonight. I can't, and I won't. Air, I need air! C'mon, let's get out of here!"

Cary and Jane watched as she left, with Matt trailing along behind her, shrugging his shoulders. Then they looked at each other and burst into laugher.

CHAPTER EIGHT

Toby liked being alone on campus, especially on such a beautiful spring evening. Listening to the music box had relaxed her, made her feel light and happy. Even the falling darkness, broken occasionally by the antique lampposts scattered about campus and lights shining from dorm windows, seemed friendly. Reluctant to leave the balmy evening to study in her room, Toby headed for the pond. She had done a lot of studying that afternoon; she could afford a few more minutes away from the books.

There was a half-moon overhead, casting a silvery glow across the water, which made it easy for Toby to see the figure that darted in and out of the pine trees. Ordinarily, Toby wouldn't have paid it that much attention. A private person herself, she wasn't a people-watcher. What other people did, she believed, was their own business. But something about the dark figure she saw caught her gaze and held it. The clothes — it was the clothing that was different. It wasn't . . . normal. It wasn't . . . now. It was *old* clothing. Very old.

Toby sat up straighter on her boulder. Of course! What was the matter with her? The long dress, the flowing hair, the cape or whatever it was called — what she was looking at was the very thing everyone on campus had been talking about — Julia Canby's ghost!

Toby jumped up. This was *very* interesting. She was, at this very moment, getting a first-hand look at the main topic of conversation at Canby Hall. True, it was very nearly dark, and not easy to see. But there was no mistaking those clothes. Wait till she told Andy! Andy knew she wasn't the sort of person to see things. And Jane would be happy as a pig in clover that someone else from Room 407 had seen Julia Canby, no matter how shadowy the vision.

"Hal-oo!" she called cheerfully.

The figure whirled, stared across the pond for a second, and then darted back into the grove of trees.

Toby shrugged. She hadn't really expected to strike up a conversation. But it never hurt to try, that was her motto. Anxious to share her exciting news with her roommates, Toby turned and ran up the slope to the main walkway, hoping Andy and Jane had returned to their room.

But Andy and Matt were walking, hand-in-hand, under the huge old oak trees, while Cary and Jane sat beside the wishing well. However, the two couples' conversations, although centered on the same subject, were very different.

"Makes sense to me," Cary was telling Jane in response to her statement about having seen Julia Canby. "All you people poking through her stuff, no wonder she's coming back from the other side to haunt you."

Jane gave him a playful smack. "We're not doing anything wrong. We're taking very good care of Julia's things. I certainly am. I turn the pages of that diary as if they were as fragile as my mother's best crystal. Besides," she added, "how do you know she's here because she's angry? Maybe she's just curious about our reaction to the exhibit. Or maybe," she added softly, "she's just lonely, like she was in London."

Cary shrugged. "Could be. They say it's usually unhappiness or anger that brings people back."

Jane shifted uncomfortably on the rock wall. "Cary, that sounds so . . . eerie. I didn't know you were an authority on the supernatural."

"I'm not." He laughed. "Actually, I don't know much about any of that stuff. But, I mean, I can't even define reality, can you?"

"I don't think about it," Jane said, laughing

ruefully. Then she sighed. "But I know Andy thinks it's just some Canby Hall student dressing up in a costume and wig, as a gag. She doesn't buy any of this stuff about ghosts!"

Toby waited impatiently in Room 407. It was already past eight-thirty and Jane and Andy were supposed to be hitting the books. So it was a gorgeous night and they were with two gorgeous guys. So what? What was more important here, romance or education? Chuckling softly to herself, Toby told the tea bag hanging over her bed, "As if I didn't know the answer to that one!" But she was so anxious to tell them about what she'd seen, she spent the next half hour pacing the little room like a caged tiger.

And she pounced on her roommates the minute they returned.

"You won't believe," Toby cried as they sank onto their beds, "what I saw down by the pond tonight. With my own two eyes!"

Andy slid backward until she was resting against her pillows. "There is something about that light in your eyes that tells me I don't want to hear this."

"Sure, you do." Toby sat down on her bed. "It's exciting!" She was silent for a moment, to build up the suspense. Then she announced with satisfaction, "I saw Julia Canby's ghost tonight!"

Andy howled and flopped over onto her

stomach, covering her head with her pillow and pounding the bed with her feet. Muffled shouts of, "No, no, no, not you, too!" emerged from beneath the pillow.

Jane laughed. "Poor Andy. She must feel like she's living all alone on an island right about now." She leaned forward, eager to hear Toby's story. "So tell me! What exactly did you see?"

Toby was totally honest. "Well, not that much, exactly. It was all sort of shadowy."

A loud "Ha!" slid out from under Andy's pillow.

"Ignore that," Jane instructed. "It's probably just a loose bedspring or something. Go *on!* I want to hear every detail."

"Well, it was the clothes that caught my eye. I mean, it was kind of dark down by the pond, but the moonlight helped. She was wearing that outfit she wears in the painting. You know, the red dress and that cape thing."

"Maroon. The dress is maroon."

"Well, whatever. Anyway, it was the same outfit. And it's not like anyone at Canby dresses that way."

"*Someone* at Canby obviously does," came the muffled voice from under the pillow on Andy's bed.

Jane directed a wicked gaze at the pillow as Toby went on. "She was on the other side of the pond, in the pine trees. And she really didn't do anything. I called to her, but it must have scared her, because she sort of giggled and skedaddled out of there."

"You *called* to her?" There was admiration in Jane's voice.

"Why not? I thought maybe if she knew I was friendly. . ."

Andy could stand it no longer. Tossing the pillow aside, she sat upright. "You," she told Toby, "have been eating locoweed. Remember, that stuff you told us about? You said it grows in fields and when animals eat it they go bonkers?"

"Andy!" Jane scolded.

"Oh, that's okay," Toby said mildly. "I guess it does sound pretty silly, trying to talk to a ghost."

"I didn't mean that! Although you've got a point. But I was talking about thinking you saw Julia Canby down by the pond."

Toby looked puzzled. "But it *was* down by the pond."

"Oh, for heaven's sake, Toby! I'm not arguing about where it was. I'm arguing about *who* it was. And it *wasn't* Julia Canby!"

Doubt clouded Toby's face. "Well, it sure looked like her. Who was it, then?"

"Anyone," Andy answered immediately. "It could have been anyone, dressing in Victorian clothing and wearing a wig. It's that simple."

There was a long silence. Andy was tired of arguing, and Jane and Toby were lost in thought. Suddenly, Jane surprised both her roommates by saying slowly, "You know, maybe Andy's got a point. It *could* be someone playing a trick on the whole school." She stood up. "And that," she said firmly, "is just the sort of stunt someone like Gigi Norton would pull! Why didn't I think of her before? She's probably mad because no one's paid any attention to her nomination for the Lit Award. So she's picked this way to get attention, not to mention upsetting the entire campus. She'd be tickled pink if we all goofed up our finals because of this ghost business, wouldn't she?"

And without thinking, Andy said, "Oh, it's not Gigi." Instantly realizing her mistake, she jumped up and went to the closet, and with her back to her roommates pretended she was searching for something.

Too late. Jane's eyes had already narrowed with suspicion, and Toby was staring at Andy intently.

"How do *you* know it couldn't be Gigi?" Jane asked. "You sounded awfully sure about that just now."

Andy just could not bring herself to admit that she'd seen the same thing they'd seen. So far, the only person who knew was Matt, and she preferred to keep it that way.

"I just meant," she said casually as she returned to her bed, "that since the descriptions have all included long, black hair, it certainly couldn't be Gigi. Her hair isn't that long."

Jane looked unconvinced. "If she could wear a costume, Andy, she could certainly wear a wig!" She hesitated, then added, "Are you hiding something? You sounded so definite, a minute ago. When you said it couldn't be Gigi, I mean."

To escape Jane's probing gaze, Andy bent down to reach under her bed for her most recent care package.

"Andy! Toby, don't you think she's acting even weirder than usual? I think she knows something about all of this ghost stuff. But I just can't believe she's keeping it to herself. Andy, what *is* it?"

But before Andy could answer, the strains of "The Skaters Waltz" began playing in the distance.

"The music box!" Toby cried. "Someone's taken it out of the library! That's against the rules. Oh, what if they break it?"

"No one's taken it from the exhibit," Andy said. "We've been hearing that music every night while you've been sleeping like, pardon the expression, the dead. It's the music Dee and Maggie asked Jane about, remember? And it's obviously just someone trying to make us think that Julia Canby is loose in these halls. Only we know better, don't we, guys?"

No answer.

"Guys? You *know* that music is part of this whole ghost stunt!"

Still no answer. Toby and Jane refused to

look at Andy. They sat on their beds, heads tilted toward the sound, eyes wide.

Andy made a face of disgust. "Well, whatever the two of you think, I, for one, am convinced that this music is just another part of this campaign to drive us all buggy. And I intend to find out where that music is coming from!"

And she jumped up and ran out of the room.

CHAPTER NINE

Although the music sounded most clearly in the hall outside Room 407, Andy could find no clues as to its origin. Determined to find its source, she knocked on every single door on the fourth floor of Baker House. All of the rooms were occupied by the students studying for finals. She received more than one curious glance as she asked the same question at every door: "Anybody in here playing 'The Skaters Waltz'?"

No one was. Still, the melody continued to play faintly. It seemed obvious to Andy that wherever its source, it could be heard more clearly in Room 407 than in the other rooms. But it seemed to be coming from nowhere. Which, Andy told herself, was, of course, impossible. She stood in the hallway outside Room 407, her eyes scanning the walls and ceiling, searching for telltale wires, for telltale anything that would lead her to the music. There was nothing. But "The Skaters Waltz" continued to tease her ears. An eerie feeling crept over her.

Shaking it off, she opened the door and rejoined her roommates. "Well, folks, I didn't solve the music's mystery," she announced. "It's kind of creepy, if you ask me. I mean, it's there, but it's *not* there, know what I mean?" She flopped down on her bed and reached for a textbook on her endtable.

"Why, Andrea Cord!" Jane said with an impish grin, "are you telling us you're beginning to believe in the supernatural?"

"I am simply telling you that there is something going on in this building. *And* on campus. And I, for one, don't think it has anything to do with the supernatural. Super-*un*natural is more like it! As creepy as that music is, I still think someone at Canby is up to no good."

"But why?" Toby asked, propping her chin on a bunched-up pillow. "Why would anyone do such an all-fired, dumb thing? Dressin' up like little Julia Canby? Playing that music at night?"

"I don't have the faintest idea. But I have every intention of finding out." Andy lay on her back, staring up at the ceiling. "I'm just not sure how. Not yet. But I'll think of something."

Almost as if it had heard her promise, the music stopped suddenly.

"You always think of something," Toby said complacently. "But while you strain your brain on this ghost stuff, I've got to get back to my science book." Lowering her voice, she muttered, "I just don't see why I need to know about sedimentary rock. I live in Texas, for gosh sakes."

Jane had already returned to her diary notes. She wasn't interested in Andy's theory that someone earthly was responsible for the ghostly goings-on. She felt a strong kinship to Julia Canby, and it was much nicer pretending, even for a little while, that perhaps Julia was closer than the pages of a leather-bound diary.

"Jane," Andy asked suspiciously, "are you studying? What about that essay for the Lit Award? Have you even started that?"

"I'm working on that right now," Jane replied. "I told you, I'm going to write about Julia. So this," she said, holding up her notes, "is research."

"Well, I still think writing an essay about a dead person is dumb."

"Nobody asked you," Jane said lazily. "And would you say that if I were writing about Faulkner or Hemingway?"

Aware that Jane had her there, Andy gave up. Jane could be so stubborn sometimes! Ignoring the fact that the same adjective could well apply to herself, Andy returned to her own studying.

Satisfied that she had made her point, Jane picked up the copy she had made of another letter written to Julia during her European vacation.

Dear Julia,

When are you coming home? Everyone is so anxious for your return, me most of all. Things just aren't the same without you. You do not sound like you're having a very good time. How can you *not* have a good time in Europe? Mama says that's just not possible. She thinks your Papa is being unfair, but I'm not supposed to tell you that. Haven't you met any boys at all? How dreary. John Ludlow comes by every single day to find out when you're returning. The poor thing! You must tell your Papa that you need to come home quickly, before someone takes pity on John and comforts him in your absence. (I'm just teasing, so don't worry). But hurry home!

Your best friend,
Clarice van der Horn

Hmm. Jane was wondering just how loyal a best friend Clarice really was. She smiled. Sadness caused by the knowledge that John Ludlow had never seen Julia alive again was eased by the suspicion that Julia's best friend, who sounded like a nice enough person, had probably taken her place in the boy's affections. Maybe they had comforted each other. It was a nice thought.

The next day after classes, Jane was summoned to Meredith's "penthouse" apartment. She arrived to find Penny Vanderark and Gigi Norton already comfortable on the little white rug in front of the fireplace. She smiled at Penny, raised an eyebrow in Gigi's direction, and took a seat on the upholstered couch, facing her classmates.

"You've probably already heard," Merrie told the girls as she took a seat beside Jane, "that the winner of the Literature Award is going to be decided by essay. I've been asked to tell all three of you since two of you are from Baker. I understand that, as usual, rumor preceded fact. So this probably comes as no surprise to any of you."

"I heard about it two days ago," Gigi announced smugly. "I've already finished a six-page outline."

"Well, isn't that just wonderful," Jane said calmly, flicking an imaginary piece of dust from her shorts. "We're so happy for you, aren't we, Penny?"

Penny nodded, a grin spreading across her face. "Yes, of course. My goodness, where would Gigi be without an outline? Where is *anyone* without an outline?"

Before Gigi could respond, Meredith realized that the conversation was getting away from her, and stepped in. "No specific topic has been assigned. You're free to choose your own. Ten pages, typed, double-spaced. Ms. Allardyce knows all three of you well enough to trust in your good taste, of course."

"Of course," Jane said soberly.

Gigi snickered rudely. "Well, *some* of us can be trusted," she said snidely. "That is, those of us who don't date rock musicians with earrings and long hair."

Unperturbed, Jane murmured, "Then there are those of us who don't date *anyone.*" Penny giggled.

"Please, girls," Merrie warned, "let's stick to the subject at hand, okay? The essays are due in exactly one week. A late paper will automatically be disqualified. I know you're busy with finals preparation right now, but those are the rules. Fair enough?"

"Fair enough," Penny agreed, her mind already tossing around several possible subjects for her essay. Math and history and science might send her mind into cartwheels, but writing was as easy as breathing. She was looking forward to it.

Jane picked at her gold watchband, wondering where on earth she was going to find the extra time necessary for the writing of this essay. Andy and Toby were counting on her to win this award for Room 407, and she would hate to let them down. True, she'd already done a lot of preliminary work, studying the diary and Julia's letters. But with the other demands on her time, she was beginning to feel pulled in ten different directions at the same time. And the problem was, she wasn't made of rubber.

And she was wasting time sitting here glaring at Gigi. She stood up. "We'll do our best, Merrie," she promised. "It's just that right now, with finals coming up, concentrating on any one thing for very long is a real challenge." She laughed without humor. "Getting all of it done is kind of like trying to dig a six-foot-deep hole armed with just a toothpick."

Merrie frowned. A look of concern spread across her face. "If you're really feeling overloaded . . ."

Jane waved a hand. "No, no, it's okay." She didn't want to worry Merrie. "It's just a matter of buckling down, that's all."

Gigi made another rude sound as Jane and Penny started for the door. "Don't strain your brain, Barrett," she said harshly. "You'll short-circuit something."

Ignoring her, Jane smiled at Merrie and thanked her for the information about the essay contest.

"If any of you needs help," their housemother said warmly, "I'll be happy to go over your rough drafts with you. Just let me know."

Thanking her again, Jane and Penny left.

Gigi was still sitting on the floor when the door closed behind them.

"I guess she didn't understand the instructions about the essay," Penny said with a grin. "She needs further clarification of the requirements."

"Yeah," Jane agreed, "as in ten pages means five pages plus five more. . . ."

Laughing, they hurried down the stairs. They were almost to Room 407 when Penny asked hesitantly, "Jane, do you think Merrie has heard any of the rumors about Julia Canby's ghost?"

The same question had occurred to Jane. "I couldn't tell. I mean, Merrie always seems to know what's happening on campus. But usually she asks us about something she's heard. If she has heard about what's going on, I guess she's not ready to say anything."

"Maybe she isn't paying that much attention to the rumors."

Jane bristled. "You mean because they're so silly?" she asked sharply.

Penny flushed. "No, I just meant . . . well, maybe she hasn't actually talked to anyone who's *seen* Julia, that's all. I guess she wouldn't take it too seriously until she's done that, don't you think?"

Jane was sorry she'd been so testy. Penny was right, of course. Until you'd actually seen Julia, or talked to someone who had, the whole thing would be hard to believe. And some people, like Andy, wouldn't pay any attention even then. But Merrie would. Wouldn't she?

Andy and Toby were waiting for them in Room 407. "Where have you guys been? Matt and Cary are waiting downstairs. Cary says he couldn't wait until our study Saturday to see you and that if he doesn't get some pizza right now, all of his beautiful long hair is going to turn gray."

Her roommates laughed.

"And he says," Andy continued, reaching for a sweater, "that you wouldn't want to date an old gray-haired guy, so you'd better get yourself downstairs fast!"

Jane glanced at her waiting textbooks and the diary notes and letters on her bed. "I *can't!*" she wailed. "I'm being held hostage by my final exams! And Merrie just officially informed us," glancing over at Penny, "that we have to write that essay for the Lit Award contest. Cary will just have to keep his hair blond without my help."

"Don't be silly, Jane," Toby said sensibly. "You have to eat. You can just spend the time at the pizza parlor instead of in the dining hall. It won't take that much longer to go into town. What's the difference?"

"Yeah," Andy added, "and if you're going to spend time on food, I really think it's illegal to choose the dining hall food over pizza."

Jane wrestled with her conscience. Her conscience lost. "Okay, okay," she yielded, "but I'm just going to eat! Then I'm coming straight home to study."

"You're not going because you're hungry," Andy said in a serious voice as the four girls left the room.

"I'm not?" Jane asked, frowning in Andy's direction.

"No. You're going because you just can't face the thought of dating a guy with gray hair. You're too shallow."

"Not true," Jane retorted without missing a step, "I'm going because if I don't, you'll eat my share of pizza. And you'll get sluggish and won't be able to dance. And I couldn't stand having a slug for a roommate." She paused a second and then added, "I'm too shallow."

Laughing, they hurried down the stairs to the waiting boys.

CHAPTER TEN

They had been seated at Pizza Pete's for several rowdy minutes when Matt turned to Andy and asked, "Seen any more ghosts?"

A shocked silence fell over the table. Jane's eyes widened, her mouth dropped open, and Toby said in a puzzled voice, "But Andy hasn't seen anything. I have, and Jane has, but not Andy."

"Yes, she has," Matt replied with certainty. "Sure, she has. Haven't you, Andy? Remember, you said you saw Julia Canby on campus."

"Andy!" Jane cried, sitting up very straight. "You've been making fun of all of us when you actually saw the ghost yourself? What a rotten thing to do! You never said a word!"

Andy's dark eyes shot daggers at an innocent Matt. "I didn't say anything," she defended herself, "because I still think you've all gone bananas. And you didn't need any more ammunition for your theory that dear old Julia was wandering around campus. Which she *isn't*. All I saw was just someone dressed up in Victorian clothing. And probably wearing a wig."

"You don't *know* that." Jane's voice was chilly. "You can't possibly *know* that." Her words gathered speed and volume. "You acted like we were all seeing things, and all the time you knew exactly what we were talking about." Her blue eyes were cold and accusing.

Andy squirmed in her seat. She hated it when Jane was right, and she had a strong feeling that this time Jane was right.

To make matters worse, Cary joined in by saying, "Yeah, Andy, you didn't say anything to me about seeing the ghost, either, when you talked to me about Jane and the others."

"I — " but Andy wasn't allowed to finish. Jane interrupted. "You talked to Cary about *me*? Andy!" She slammed her menu down on the table. "I don't believe this! How could you?"

"Andy," Toby added, hurt in her voice, "why didn't you tell us you saw the ghost, too?"

"There *is* no ghost!" Andy cried angrily. People at other tables stared at her. She flushed and lowered her voice. "What *is* the matter with all of you? This is exactly why I didn't say anything. Because you're all acting as if it means something, and it doesn't."

As if she hadn't spoken, Penny said softly, "Gee, I can't believe you saw her, too."

"I saw a *person!*" Andy hissed vehemently. "That's all, just a person. And Jane," turning to face her roommate, whose face was an icy mask, "I talked to Cary because I thought he might help. The whole campus was going nuts. I needed help." She cast an unkind glance in Cary's direction. "But of course he was no help at all. I should have known better than to approach someone who believes in life on other planets."

"That's called having an open mind," Jane said caustically. "Something *you* would know absolutely nothing about."

"Yes, I do," Andy defended herself. "But there is no ghost of Julia Canby!"

An awkward silence descended upon the table as a waitress arrived. She stood uncertainly, aware that all was not well with the group.

"So!" she said in a hearty voice, order pad in her hands, "what'll it be?"

"Nothing!" Andy declared, standing up. Everyone stared at her as she grabbed at Matt's arm, urging him upward. "I've lost my appetite. C'mon, Matt, let's go. We'll walk."

"Andy . . ."

She tugged harder on his arm. "*C'mon!* I do *not* want to spend my evening talking about things that go bump in the night. Now, are you coming or not?"

He wasn't about to let her walk all the way home alone. Glancing around at what had become four very grim faces, he said quietly, "See you guys later." Then, without another word, he followed Andy out of the restaurant.

"So, you guys going to order or what?" the waitress asked. When no one answered, she shrugged and left, saying she'd return later.

Jane, Cary, Toby, and Penny sat lost in silence. "Wow," Cary finally said, shaking his head, "this ghost business really has Andy all fired up, doesn't it?"

"She's afraid everyone will be too flustered to do a good job on their finals," Toby said in Andy's defense.

"I just cannot believe," Jane said heatedly, "that she saw it, too, and never even told us!" Turning to Toby, she added, "And I just thought of something. Remember when she said the ghost wasn't Gigi Norton? Remember how certain she sounded? That must have been the day she saw Julia's ghost." She frowned. "But I wonder how Gigi is inolved?" Her lips tightened grimly. "We're going to have to talk to Andy the minute we get home tonight."

"If she's still speaking to us," Penny commented soberly. "She was pretty upset when she dragged Matt out of here."

"Well," Cary said cheerfully, "I'm going to be a lot more upset if I don't get some pizza pretty soon. Isn't that why we came here? I can't carry on a conversation on an empty stomach."

"Me neither," Penny agreed, and she signaled to the waitress to return.

Matt had a hard time keeping up with Andy's long, angry strides back to Canby Hall. "I am *so* tired," she complained as they hurried through the twilight, "of this silly ghost business. No one is studying for finals, there are all these crazy stories all around campus and now my roommates, who used to be sane, rational people, are mad at me."

"Well, you were pretty upset," Matt said in an effort to calm her down. "Back at the restaurant, I mean. I guess I shouldn't have opened my big mouth, right? About you seeing the ghost, I mean. I just figured you'd already told them. You always tell them everything."

"It's not your fault." Andy was beginning to calm down. "I should have told you I hadn't said anything to them. Stop blaming yourself, Matt. None of this has anything to do with you."

"Maybe not." He took her hand and held it as they walked. "But I want to help. What can I do?"

Andy shook her head. "Nothing. I don't even know what *I* can do. I guess I'm going to have to really wrestle with this one. Maybe if I strain the old brain, I can come up with some truly brilliant way to fix things."

Matt squeezed her hand. "Piece of cake. We both know you're just naturally brilliant."

Andy smiled. "You don't think you might be just a little bit prejudiced?"

"Of course not," he said lightly, putting an arm around her shoulders. "I never let personal feelings affect my judgment about a person's brilliance!"

When a subdued group of four arrived shortly thereafter on the Canby Hall campus, Jane went straight to the library. The only thing that would satisfy Andy and ease some of this stupid tension was finishing the Lit Award essay. That should make the girl relax! To do that, Jane needed to delve into Julia's diary and letters. Giving Cary an absentminded kiss good-bye, she hurried away.

He watched her go before turning to Toby and Penny. "I'm beginning to see what Andy's so uptight about. Jane doesn't seem to be of this earth right now, does she?"

"I thought you approved of her interest in Julia Canby," Toby said, surprise in her voice.

"Oh, I do." Cary grinned. "I guess I just didn't expect so much competition from a bunch of ectoplasm."

Penny laughed. "Maybe you're losing your touch, Cary."

It was his turn to laugh. "You could be right. Who knows? What I do know is, if I don't get at the books, the ghost of Canby Hall is going to be the least of my worries. See you guys later."

Penny and Toby exchanged doubtful glances when Cary's car had pulled away. "You think Andy's got a point?" Penny asked as they ascended the stone steps of Baker House. "I thought Jane was reading the diary because of her essay. She just doesn't seem the type to go overboard over something as far-out as a ghost."

"Well, don't forget," Toby responded, holding open the heavy wooden door, "Jane's a writer. At least, that's what she wants to be, if she can talk her father out of insisting that she be an investment banker. Being a writer means that Jane sees things we don't see, imagines things in her head that aren't real to us. So I guess it's not so surprising that she can feel close to Julia Canby."

"As long as she doesn't get *too* close," Penny said thoughtfully. "Andy's right about one thing. The real world still exists, and it's full of finals and the essay contest. And Cary. Jane needs to concentrate on those, too."

Shaking their heads, the girls went inside.

In the library, Jane wasn't concentrating on the real world. She was reading Julia Canby's diary entry of February 12, 1897.

Dear Diary,

I think I shall die! Edward Lynch did come, after all, but it's all so horrid! He brought me violets, my favorites, and Papa became so angry and made him leave. He said I was too young for callers and he told Edward never to come back to this hotel. I shall never see him again. I hate London! And I hate this horrible rain. Sometimes I think I even hate Papa, and I know that's a terrible thing to say. I can't help it.

My throat is scratchy, probably from crying for hours, and my head hurts. I want to go home, to my beautiful Massachusetts. I want to see Clarice and my friends. And I want to have fun again!

It's awfully warm in here, Diary. I'm going to ask Mathilde to open a window and then I'm going to bed. Because I feel too horrid and sad to do anything else.

Jane fingered the faded, withered violets crushed between two pages of the diary. She had just read the last entry in the little book. Julia's throat hadn't been sore just from crying. She'd been ill and hadn't known it.

Jane sat by the window, the little leather book in her lap, tears in her eyes. She knew she should go back to the beginning of the book and learn more about Julia's life before the European trip in order to begin her essay.

But Jane just couldn't do it at that moment. Julia in Europe, her unhappiness spilling across the pages of the diary, was still too real.

I know how she felt, she thought, surprising herself. I *shouldn't* know. My mother is alive and my father didn't drag me off to Europe alone and my parents never told me I couldn't see a boy I liked a lot. But I still know how she feels. It's almost as though she's right here, telling me what it was like for her.

And at that precise moment, a black cloak floated by the window, catching Jane's gaze.

The diary thudded to the floor as Jane jumped to her feet, her mouth open, eyes wide with shock. Stooping quickly to grab the book, she raced with it to the glass case, placed it inside and whirled to race out the door. She rounded the corner of the library in time to see a corner of the maroon dress disappear behind a tool shed. Darkness was rapidly approaching, but she could still see clearly enough to trust her own vision.

"Julia!" she called frantically, "Wait! Please wait!" Heart pounding, she ran to the tool shed. But there was no sign of a Victorian girl or anyone else.

Get a grip on yourself, Jane scolded silently as disappointment washed over her. What on earth would Andy say if she heard you calling out to a ghost? Hadn't Toby said that she'd done the same thing, called out to the vision she'd seen? And Andy had hooted.

I'm not going to tell them I saw her this time, she thought with certainty. I can't stand one more argument about this, and that's exactly what would happen if I ran into the room and shouted that I'd just seen Julia again. And Andy would make it all sound like a bad horror movie.

No, she'd keep quiet this time. Besides, she hadn't actually seen anything but a corner of the cloak and an edge of the dress. Andy certainly wouldn't buy that as evidence of anything but an overactive imagination.

Just button your lips, Jane, she told herself as she made her way across campus, and keep them that way.

But it wasn't easy, because she wasn't the only one who had seen Julia this time. Her classmates were gathered, here and there in little groups in front of their houses, chattering excitedly. Jane wasn't sure about what until a girl in her English class called out, "Hey Barrett, did you see her?"

Although Jane suspected she knew the answer to that question, she asked lightly, "See who?"

"Julia Canby, silly! She's been running around campus all evening like she owned the place."

"Well, she *did*, once," Jane replied in a slightly shaky voice, "remember?"

The girl laughed and turned back to her companions as Jane hurried on. Her mind was reeling. So she hadn't been the only one to see Julia. Others had seen her, too. Would that carry any weight with Andy? Probably not. She'd just say everyone was crazy.

Jane hurried up to Room 407. Talk about being stressed out! They had enough on their minds with finals coming up without all of this added tension. The last thing they needed right now was arguing among themselves over just how close to them Julia Canby really was. Maybe if they discussed it, openly and honestly, they could send all of this unpleasantness packing, for good. They could at least try.

Filled with resolve, she opened the door to her room.

A nosegay of violets was lying on her bed.

CHAPTER ELEVEN

Jane stared at the bouquet with disbelieving eyes. A line from the diary rang in her ears: "He brought me violets, my favorites."

What were those violets doing on her bed?

Her gaze slid from the bed to her roommates, who were silently standing by their own beds. "How did *this* get here?" she asked, pointing to the nosegay.

Dual shrugs. "It was there when I came in," Andy said. Toby nodded.

"You didn't *see* anyone? No one left a message?"

"I *said*," Andy replied a little testily, "it was sitting there when I came in. Don't you believe me?"

"Of course, I do!" Jane sat down on her bed and picked up the nosegay. The delicate violets were bunched closely together, their stems wrapped in pale blue tissue paper, a pale blue ribbon wound around the paper.

There was a dainty white lace collar between the stems and the blossoms. There was no card, no tag, no way of knowing who had given her flowers. But then, there wouldn't be, if the bouquet was meant as a prank.

But who would do that? Someone who wanted to ridicule her interest in Julia? Someone who thought she was wasting her time with the diary? Was someone making fun of her?

Holding the bouquet in her hands, she lifted her gaze and focused on Andy. "You *really* don't know anything about these flowers, do you, Andy?"

Andy stood up very straight. "What's that supposed to mean?"

Jane kept her eyes on Andy's face. "You might think this would make a good joke."

Andy's face registered bewilderment. "Joke? What's funny about flowers?"

Her confusion seemed genuine. But Jane was not convinced. Andy hadn't told them she'd seen Julia Canby, had she? So maybe she'd just neglected to tell them that she'd heard Julia Canby's favorite flower was the violet. Delivering the nosegay might be her way of pointing out how ridiculous she thought Jane's interest in the diary was. She'd certainly said so a thousand times!

"These were Julia Canby's favorite flowers," she said clearly, watching Andy carefully. There! Wasn't that uneasiness in her face a sure sign of guilt? Andy had probably picked up the bouquet after she and Matt left the restaurant. After all, she *had* been angry with Jane when she left.

Andy frowned, unable to read the expression on Jane's face. "So? You're the only person in this room who knew that."

"Am I?" Jane asked, standing up. "Am I really?"

This time there was no mistaking the implication in Jane's words.

"You think *I* bought those flowers?" Andy's voice grew taut. "Why would I do that?"

"To teach me some sort of stupid lesson, maybe?" Jane said harshly. "Or maybe just to make fun of my interest in Julia Canby." But she was already regretting her accusation. Andy really didn't seem to have the faintest idea where the flowers had come from. She was a good actress, but she wasn't that good. She probably didn't know anything about the bouquet.

"Are you serious?" Andy's body grew as stiff and rigid as a pole as the meaning of Jane's remark registered. "You think I'd try to psych you out like that? Boy, you really have gone off the deep end!"

Jane had been teetering on the brink of apology. But Andy's remark sent Jane's temper soaring again.

"You've been making fun of my interest in Julia Canby and the exhibit from the start, and I'm sick of it! Just because I care about something you're not interested in doesn't make me wrong *or* silly *or* stupid *or* crazy! And *this*," tossing the nosegay on her bed in disgust, "is just the worst. The worst!" And she turned and ran out of the room, slamming the door so hard the tea bag over Toby's bed did a little dance.

"Oh, boy," Toby breathed, "we sure seem to be going from bad to worse, don't we?"

"You can say that again," Andy agreed, sinking down on her bed, staring glumly at the bouquet. "How could she think I'd pull a stunt like that? I wouldn't do something like that, and she knows it. At least, she should! Besides, I *didn't* know about the violets and Julia. How would I? You believe me, don't you?"

Toby nodded. "Sure. You wouldn't lie about it."

"Well, thanks. I wish Jane was as sure of that as you are."

Toby sat down on the floor, long legs stretched out in front of her. "I think she is. I could tell she was sorry almost as soon as she said those things."

"Oh, right. I could *see* that!"

Toby ignored the sarcasm. "No, I mean it. But you know Jane. She never learned how to backtrack. She's no good at eating her words."

Andy shook her head. "I don't know. I

guess you could be right. But she sure sounded like she was convinced I'd played this trick on her." She thought for a moment before adding slowly, "Well, *we* know I didn't put violets on Jane's bed. The question is, who *did*?"

"That reminds me," Toby said abruptly, surprising Andy, "the other day you said the ghost couldn't be Gigi Norton. Jane and I wondered how you knew that."

"I saw her. I saw Gigi right after I saw the ghost. So I knew it couldn't be Gigi dressing up in Julia's clothes."

"Couldn't she have changed into regular clothes after you saw Julia?"

Andy shook her head. "No. There wasn't time. It just wasn't her, that's all. And boy, was I disappointed! I'd already convinced myself she had to be behind the whole thing." She chewed on her lower lip. "But it's *some-one*. There *is* no ghost. And," as she stood up, "I have to find out who it is. The whole school is practically hysterical, sure that Julia Canby is running around campus and playing music at night. If someone doesn't put an end to this, finals are going to be an absolute disaster. P.A. will have all our heads if a parade of C's and D's marches across her grade lists."

Toby nodded soberly. She hadn't yet achieved an understanding of sedimentary rock for science class herself.

"Now," Andy continued, "you and I both know there is no ghost."

Toby gave her a look that clearly said, We do?

Andy repeated, "There is *no* ghost, Toby. Which means that someone on this campus is playing tricks on everyone else. We have to find out who is dressing up in Victorian clothes and playing this stupid game. It's not funny. And playing music late at night — that isn't on the top forty list of hits — isn't very funny, either. We need," Andy finished with determination, "to do some heavy detective work." Walking over to Jane's bed, she reached down and picked up the nosegay. "I think," she said slowly, "that this is one Canby Hall student who's going to skip that day of study we planned for Saturday."

"But it was your idea!"

"I know. But some things are more important." Tapping the bouquet against her hand, she said, "I have to go into town."

"I'm going with you."

"No, you stay here. You need to learn about rocks."

Toby knew Andy was right. But the rocks would just have to wait. Some things, as Andy said, were more important. "If what you're going to do in town is going to help make things better on this campus, I'm included, Andy. And I don't want any hassle about it. I'm going, and that's final."

Andy could always tell when Toby meant business. "Okay, okay. Maybe I can help you study sometimes over the weekend. But we can't do anything about anything tonight. So I'm going to study for a while, then crash. Why don't you go hunting for Jane? She can't spend the night in the hall. Tell her I won't utter one single word about hobgoblins or ghosts, I promise."

And so, on Saturday morning, while Jane was still searching through her overloaded closet for the perfect outfit for a day of study, Andy and Toby headed for town, saying they needed essentials like shampoo and nail polish. Jane was too preoccupied to be suspicious.

There was only one florist shop in town. The owner was friendly and cooperative.

"Sure, I remember selling that nosegay," she said in answer to the girls' inquiry. "I don't get many orders like that one. Kind of old-fashioned, know what I mean? But I can't tell you who bought them. She paid cash, so I don't have a check with a name and address on it."

"She?" Andy had thought it might have been Cary who sent the flowers, although it wasn't at all like him not to sign his name to a gift.

"Yes, it was a young girl. I remember that much."

Andy sent Toby a look. It said, Now we're getting somewhere. "What did the girl look like?"

"Oh, tall, thin, long dark hair." She couldn't remember any more than that, so Andy and Toby left, thanking her for her help.

As they walked along the main street in the tiny village, the sun on their faces, Toby remarked that the description actually sounded a lot like, well, like Julia Canby.

"Or Gigi Norton with a wig," Andy said sharply. "And this is just the sort of low-life stunt she'd pull. I don't care if I *did* see her that day, I still have a feeling she's behind all of this. At any rate, it would sure be a lot easier for Gigi to buy violets than it would for Julia. At least Gigi's *alive*. Although," she finished grimly, "maybe not for long if she really is causing all this trouble at school!"

"Wow, I'm glad *I'm* not Gigi Norton," Toby said gratefully.

Andy laughed. "You're not the only one. Since you're *not* Norton, I'll treat you to a Coke. C'mon."

At Canby Hall, Jane and Cary, with Matt, Penny, Dee and Maggie, and a dozen or so other Canby and Oakley students were gathered together on blankets spread across the green expanse of lawn, surrounded by picnic baskets and Styrofoam coolers. Opened books and notebooks decorated each of the blankets. Between the constant moaning and groaning about finals, remarks flew about the ghost of Canby Hall. Some were casual, uttered in a joking way. Others, like Jane's, were completely serious.

"She really was unhappy in London," she told Cary. "It just doesn't seem fair. Why couldn't her father see that? Or didn't he care?"

"I'm sure he cared," Cary said matter-of-factly, although he'd read none of the diary. "The guy probably just had other things on his mind, that's all. More important things."

"What's more important than a man's daughter?" Jane said grumpily, but Cary had already turned away.

"Where's Andy?" Dee wanted to know. "This was her idea, and she's not even here."

"She said she had to go to town," Jane replied. "Toby, too. Seemed strange to me. After all, Andy was the one who talked me into this. Now all of a sudden buying shampoo is more important than studying for finals? And she calls *me* crazy!"

Two girls came out of Baker House just then, arm in arm. One of them was Gigi Norton. The other was a tall, thin girl with long black hair.

Jane drew her breath in sharply. "Isn't that Agnes Pearl with Gigi?"

Dee looked up. "Oh — yeah. From what I hear, she's been hanging around with Norton a lot lately."

"I've never really noticed her before. She lives at the other end of our hall — what's she like?"

Dee grinned. "Ever heard of the expression about birds of a feather flocking together? They're two of a kind. The only reason Pearl can tolerate Norton, and vice versa, is that they're exactly alike. No one I know at Baker *or* at Addison House can stand good old Agnes — except she's a lot quieter than Gigi."

"Hmm —"

"Why are you so interested?" Dee asked.

Jane hesitated. She didn't want to bring up Julia again. The subject seemed to make people uncomfortable. They just didn't understand. But at least Andy wasn't around to shriek when the words "Julia Canby" escaped from Jane's lips. "Well, it's just that for a second there, when they first came out of Baker, I thought that girl with Gigi looked just like Julia Canby."

"Oh, yeah? Gee, I don't see it." Dee shook her head. "She's not pretty at all. Agnes, I mean. I think Julia's pretty, don't you, Maggie? In her portrait, I mean."

"Well, I know," Jane said quickly, "I know Julia's prettier. But, just for a minute there. . . ."

They watched in silence as the two girls walked toward the pond. Then Dee turned to Jane, grinning. "Oh, I get it! You think the ghost could be Agnes dressing up as Julia."

Jane said nothing. The thought *had* crossed her mind. And it was an idea Andy would love. A logical, rational explanation for the appearances of the girl in the portrait.

"Well, forget it," Dee said. "It crossed my mind, too, when you said that just now about how much they look alike. But I know for a fact that Agnes was in her room twice when Julia was spotted on campus. She came running to her door when the person who had seen the ghost came through the hall like the town crier, shouting that she'd seen Julia Canby. There was Agnes, big as life, standing in her doorway. I saw her with my own eyes, and this was only seconds after the ghost had been seen. So, no way, Jane. Sorry."

Although Dee expected Jane to be disappointed, she was, in fact, relieved. It would have been so awful if Agnes Pearl had been the Julia Canby everyone had seen. Just awful! So awful that Jane couldn't stand to think about it.

Turning away from Dee, Jane concentrated on her textbooks.

CHAPTER TWELVE

An uneasy peace lay over Room 407 that evening. Everyone had decided to spend Saturday night studying. All three girls had settled in for the night, dressed in pajamas and robes, ready for a few final hours of study. But they were all concentrating more on trying to ignore the tension in the room than on their textbooks.

They deliberately didn't mention many things. Andy and Toby kept their visit to town to themselves. Jane said nothing at all about the new friend she'd seen with Gigi, although at one point, she thought about it. Maybe Toby or Andy knew something about Agnes Pearl. But bringing up Agnes could mean another discussion about the one subject they were all trying so hard to ignore: Julia Canby. She decided to say nothing.

Andy helped Toby work on her science material. Watching them, Jane felt resentment growing inside her like heartburn. Toby, after all, had talked about a ghost, too — that old miner she'd mentioned. Why wasn't Andy making an issue of that?

The evening crept by, until it was nearly time for bed.

Then the melody began to play, but this time Andy was more than ready. She jumped up, startling her roommates. "Okay, guys, that does it! I've had it with that stupid tune! Anyone with any brains at all could figure out that someone taped it right from the music box and then hid the tape recorder where we could hear it but not see it. And I'm going to find it if I have to turn this building upside-down!"

"Oh, marvelous," Jane scoffed. "You don't have a shred of proof that someone did such a thing, and you're going to start hunting for a tape recorder? If I didn't know better, Andy, I'd think you'd been watching too much television."

The music, Andy noticed, sounded closer this time. "Well, I haven't," she snapped. "And . . ." she lifted her head to listen carefully for a second or two . . . "I wouldn't be surprised if that music was coming from somewhere in this very room."

"In *our* room?" Toby, a look of alarm on her face, sat up in bed. "Some strange person has been in our room?"

"Toby, calm down," Jane ordered. "Andy

doesn't know any such thing ever happened. She can't possibly be sure."

"Sure enough to conduct a thorough search," Andy retorted.

"Conduct a thorough search?" Jane laughed. "You *have* been watching too much television. I just can't figure out where or when." Then she added slyly, "But then, I'm not a great detective like you."

"Very funny, Jane." Andy began stripping her bed. "I know that thing is in here somewhere. I'm going over every inch of this room."

Jane cried, "Not *my* inches, you're not! You're not going to make a mess of my stuff just because of your silly suspicions."

Andy whirled around to stare at her. "Make a mess of your things? Jane, how could I? Your stuff is *already* a mess. Anyway, all I'm going to do is look through it."

"No, you're not."

"Yes, I am."

"No!"

"Yes!"

Their stalemate could have gone on, but the music suddenly stopped.

"There!" Andy declared triumphantly, "did you hear that? That was a definite click!" She aimed a level gaze at Jane. "As in the click of a tape recorder shutting off."

"I didn't hear a thing."

"Toby? You heard it, didn't you?"

Toby shook her head. "I'm sorry, Andy. All I heard was you and Jane arguing."

Turning away from them in disgust, Andy continued the search of her own area. But without the melody to guide her, she had no idea where to look. Giving up, she sank down on the bed she had just re-made. "I *am*," she announced, "going to get to the bottom of this. But searching all of Baker House is not the answer."

But no one was paying any attention to her. Jane was lost in the diary notes and Toby was writing a letter to Neal, telling him about all of the weird happenings at Canby Hall.

"Well, I can see I'm not getting any help here," Andy commented. She got up and left the room, not exactly sure where she was going. It was just too frustrating sitting in the same room with two people who didn't share her concern about the things that were happening. Maybe she could find someone who did.

It wasn't going to be Matt, she found out when she called Oakley Prep. "Gee, I'm sorry, Andy, I really am, but I can't talk right now. I'm helping Cary with a science experiment. Call you tomorrow, okay?"

Andy hung up, disappointed. She was on her own. Oh, well, she thought, it's not the first time and it probably won't be the last. I could probably talk Toby into helping, but she's having so much trouble with science, she can't afford the time. Besides, playing detective might be fun.

And someone was going to have to do it if Canby Hall was going to get back to normal and finals weren't going to be a total disaster — someone was going to have to prove that Julia Canby's ghost wasn't on campus.

Lying awake later in a quiet room, she went over all of the "detection" tactics she had learned from television. Of all of them, the only approach that seemed the least bit plausible was one that was always called surveillance. She would *follow* Gigi.

I'll hang on her like a shadow, she told herself, until I either find out she's innocent, which of course she isn't, or I catch her in the act. I'll trail after her like ivy, and she'll never know I'm there.

She was wondering if it would be too warm to wear a trench coat the next day when she fell asleep.

In the morning, a beautiful, fresh Sunday, they narrowly avoided another argument.

"What's everybody doing today?" Jane asked sleepily, rubbing her eyes. Andy was already dressed, in pale blue shorts and a matching long-sleeved sweatshirt, and Toby, up and showered an hour earlier, was making her bed.

"I'm going to take a hike in the woods to clear my brain," Toby answered. "Then I guess I'll be doing some more studying. Outside. I'm not staying inside on a pretty day like this."

"Me, neither," Andy agreed. But she offered no more than that, and no one pressed her further. "How about you, Jane?" Neither of them had apologized for the previous evening's disagreement. But now that Andy had formulated a definite plan of action, she felt forgiving. "You planning to study? Or work on your essay? Or," generously, "are you just going to relax?"

"Relax? Ha! Don't I wish! I have to work on my essay. But I agree with both of you. I'm *not* going to do it inside. If I have to spend the day working, I can at least improve my tan at the same time."

"Me, too," Andy said, her expression blank. Jane and Toby laughed.

Still, in spite of the laughter, there was an undercurrent of tension in the room. They all felt it. Each was making a concentrated effort to avoid *the* subject. Andy solved the problem by leaving. She was anxious to get started on what she thought of as her "project." If Gigi wasn't up yet, Andy planned to wait in the dining hall until she showed up. Then her detecting could officially begin.

It *was* too warm for a trench coat. Too obvious, anyway, she decided cheerfully as she hurried across the campus to the dining hall.

She had had two cups of cocoa and three glasses of juice by the time Gigi Norton entered the dining hall — alone. Andy had found waiting all that time difficult and wondered why detective work looked so exciting on television. It wasn't just the sitting still that she found annoying in the dining hall, it was the conversation around her as well. Every girl she spoke to had only one thing on her mind: Julia Canby's appearances on the Canby Hall campus. Each time she tried to change the subject by asking, "So. You ready for finals?" the person she was addressing would look blank.

Scary, Andy thought, really scary. Finals at Canby had definitely taken a backseat to an apparition. Well, at least *one* person intended to do something about it. If Andy'd had any doubts about what she was doing, they were gone now. It was time everyone remembered exactly why they'd come to this school in the first place.

If I don't find what I'm looking for, she thought with certainty, poking with her fork at dried egg on her plate, everyone's going to flunk. The grade list is going to look as if a little kid's been practicing writing the letter *F*. P.A. will have a fit, the school will be closed, and we'll all be sent home in disgrace.

Then Gigi arrived and Andy's natural optimism returned. I won't fail at this, she told herself with new resolve. I *can't*.

Toby came in, her face flushed from her hike. "What are you doing sitting here all by yourself?" she asked. "And why are you staring at Gigi like that?"

"I'm sitting here alone because it's the only way to avoid hearing everything I never wanted to know about ghosts." She said nothing about why she was staring at Gigi.

"Then you'd better skedaddle out of here before Jane gets here. Her head is just full of information about Julia, all that stuff she's learned for her essay. She probably won't be able to talk about anything else, and then you'll get mad, and then you two will argue again."

Andy wasn't willing to have another argument with Jane. She jumped up. No point in taking any chances. Now that she knew where Gigi was, she'd wait for her outside. There must be a pine tree or tall bush she could hide behind. Anything was better than getting into another hassle with one of her roommates.

She found an obliging pine tree and disappeared behind it. She kept her eyes on the dining hall door and was ready for Gigi when she emerged a few minutes later.

The conclusion Andy came to after only one hour of playing shadow to Gigi was that the girl led an extremely boring life. Another was that television really did make things look much more glamorous than they really were. *And* easier. She had little difficulty "tailing" Gigi outside, where the campus was

lush with greenery to hide behind. But when
Gigi went up to Agnes Pearl's room in Baker
House, things became more difficult. The halls
were long and empty, with no place to hide.
So Andy had to stay so far behind Gigi, she
was sure she would lose her.

She didn't. Her biggest challenge became
fighting off boredom. Gigi simply ate breakfast alone and went to Baker House, where she
went into Agnes's room and closed the door.
Andy was tempted at that point to forget the
whole thing and go about her own business.
But she reminded herself sternly that this *was*
her business and it was important.

So she took up a position behind a potted
palm at one end of the corridor. From that
vantage point, she could see Agnes's door
clearly. The few people who passed by never
noticed Andy, too busy chattering to check
behind greenery that was a normal fixture in
the hall.

After a long, uncomfortable twenty minutes of palm fronds tickling her nose, Andy
saw the door to Agnes's room open. Gigi
emerged. Andy watched as Gigi went straight
to the broom closet, opened the door and went
inside. A few minutes later she came back out
and returned to Agnes's room, empty-handed.

Andy knew that the fourth-floor broom
closet was often used by Baker House girls as a
spot for a little "private time," especially
when they were depressed or upset about

something. Gigi didn't seem to be depressed *or* upset. But then, who could tell about Gigi? Most of the time, her expression was so bland it was impossible to tell what she was thinking. Or if she was thinking anything at all.

She made two more identical trips while Andy watched. Into the broom closet, back out and into Agnes's room, then back to the broom closet and out again.

When the door to the room had closed behind her for a third time, Andy leaned against the wall behind the potted palm, frowning.

Why was Gigi Norton spending so much time in the Baker House broom closet?

Andy was pretty sure she had the answer to that question.

CHAPTER THIRTEEN

When Jane joined Toby in the dining hall, her first question was, "Where's Andy? I thought she came over here."

"She did. But she left." Toby avoided Jane's eyes. "I guess she had things to do."

"You mean she didn't want to listen to me ramble on about Julia Canby. You mean she's had it with ghost-talk."

Toby laughed. "Yeah, I guess. Don't be mad. Andy's just so . . . down-to-earth. This . . . supernatural stuff is hard on her."

Jane stirred her oatmeal, hoping the lumps would disappear. They remained, little lumps of rock in a beige desert. "I know. And she's right about one thing: It's really hard to concentrate on finals or anything else when there might be a ghost on campus."

Toby tilted her head. "Might be? You mean you're not sure?"

"Sure? A ghost isn't something anyone can

be *sure* of, Toby." She paused before adding, "I want Julia to be real because I know so much about her now. I feel very close to her. But I'm not stupid. I know it's not possible."

"You do?"

Jane laughed. "Well, kind of. I *do* agree with Andy that something's going on, though. I just can't imagine what."

"Andy still thinks it's Gigi."

"What? I thought she said it couldn't possibly be Gigi. And we never did find out why she said that, did we?"

"I did. She told me that she saw Gigi right after she saw the ghost. I thought maybe Gigi had time to change her clothes, but Andy said there was no way."

Jane's face fell. "Well, if it isn't Gigi, then who?"

"I don't know." Toby put her empty milk carton on her tray and stood up. "But I think Andy intends to find out."

"Without *us*? Aren't we all in this together?"

"I guess she thought we wouldn't help after all the arguments we've had about the ghost."

Jane's tanned cheeks flushed pink. "You mean after all the arguing *I* did."

Toby shook her head. "It was me, too, and lots of other girls here. And I'm still not about to say for sure there's no such thing as a ghost at Canby Hall. 'Cause I can't know that for sure, can I? And that makes Andy mad. That's why she didn't ask for my help."

"Maybe you're right. I wonder how she plans to figure out what's going on, if something is, and who's behind it?" She laughed as she stood up. "Think she's wearing a trench coat while she does her detective work?"

Toby grinned. "Nah. Too warm for that."

Gigi had finally left Baker. Andy hurried to the broom closet and went in. Turning the lock, she settled down to methodically and thoroughly search the closet. She knew exactly what she was hunting for: a tape recorder and some Victorian clothing and a wig.

She found the tape recorder first. It was hidden behind several large boxes of laundry detergent. Setting it on the floor and pressing the Play button, she listened for a few seconds. She wasn't at all surprised to hear "The Skaters Waltz." So, she was on the right track. Triumphantly grinning, she turned off the music and continued searching.

"Aha!" she cried a few minutes later, unearthing a bundle of clothing from a pile of dust rags in a corner. She held in her hands a maroon dress and a black cloak. "Good grief!" she muttered, "I hope she's going to iron these before she wears again. They're a mess!"

The wig was behind a group of tissue boxes. Andy had no doubt that it, along with the clothing, had more or less been borrowed from the Canby Hall Drama Department.

She sat down on the floor, wondering what she should do with the evidence she'd found. There was no proof that the items had been hidden there by one Gigi Norton. Unless she caught Gigi actually dressing in the outfit, what she had found was no proof at all. Anyone could use the broom closet for privacy, and almost everyone did.

"But, at least," she said aloud, holding the wig in her hands, "I found out for myself. I know now that Gigi *is* behind the ghost of Canby Hall. The question is, how do I convince everyone else?"

Replacing the wig and clothing, she returned to her own room. She sat at the desk by the window, looking out over the sunny green campus. What a gorgeous day! If only everything was as great as the weather. . . .

Jane and Toby came in, chattering about the weather, too. "I don't know about anyone else," Jane said, "but I'm taking a blanket and my books and heading for the great outdoors."

"Me, too!" Toby agreed.

"I found the clothes," Andy said abruptly.

Her roommates continued gathering together personal belongings. "Clothes?" Toby asked, "what clothes?"

"Will you *stop* what you're doing and listen? This is important!"

Startled, they turned to face her.

"I found the clothes our so-called ghost has been wearing. And the wig. And a tape recorder. The song it plays is the tune from the music box. I found all of it in the broom closet." She was almost sorry she'd announced her news when she saw the look on Jane's face. There was such disappointment in that look. She was hoping, Andy thought uncomfortably, she was really hoping Julia was real. She knew better, but she was still hoping.

"You did?"

"Yes. And I think they're Gigi's. She must have confiscated them from the Drama Department. Remember, they did *The Importance of Being Ernest* last year? The clothes are probably from that. The wig could be from anything."

"I'm confused," Jane said, sitting down on her bed. "You were so sure before that it couldn't be Gigi. And Gigi lives in Addison! What changed your mind?"

Andy frowned. "Well, I still haven't figured out what happened that day I saw . . . the ghost. But I just know there's an explanation. Because Gigi is the one who led me to the broom closet when I was watching her this morning — "

"Watching her?"

"Yes, and don't interrupt. I was watching her, and I've got to tell you, that girl leads the most boring life! It looks like Agnes Pearl is her only friend."

"Yes, but Agnes is a significant friend," Jane said.

"What?" Andy looked annoyed at this second interruption.

"Agnes — she looks a lot like — "

This time, Andy did the interrupting. "Never mind all that," she said impatiently. "She wasn't with anyone when I was watching her. But she made three trips to the broom closet. Not for privacy — she didn't stay long enough. So when she finally left the building, I checked in there. And there they were! The clothes, the wig, and the tape recorder. Gigi's weapons in the fight against Canby Hall's sanity."

"What are you going to do?" Toby asked as Jane let Andy's words sink in.

"I don't know yet. I can't prove that Gigi left all that stuff there. It could have been hidden there by anyone."

Jane was shaking her head. Suddenly, she jumped to her feet. "I don't want to talk about this anymore," she cried. "It's just too much! Whatever you do, leave me out of it. Just leave me out of it!"

Andy looked up at her in surprise. "This involves you, too! I thought you'd be glad we found out who was behind our *ghost*."

"Well, I'm not!" Jane stood in front of the door, her arms full of books, her body stiff. "I just can't stand your smugness, Andrea Cord! You're just pleased as punch that there isn't really any ghost. That it's someone right here on campus."

"Well, of course it's someone right here on campus. Who *else* would it be?"

The look on Jane's face confirmed Andy's earlier suspicions: that even in Jane's most logical moments, she had still held out a shred of hope that her feeling of closeness to Julia Canby hadn't been only in her imagination. Andy's discoveries in the broom closet had destroyed that hope.

Andy felt sorry for Jane. But she didn't think it was very fair that she was getting yelled at for finding out the truth. "Jane, I'm sorry." She spread her hands helplessly in front of her. "But we needed to know — "

"*I* didn't," Jane snapped. And she whirled and yanked open the door. Then she was gone, leaving Andy and Toby staring at each other in dismay.

"I don't understand," Toby said softly. "When we talked about it, she sounded like she already knew there wasn't any real ghost. Why is she so upset?"

Andy shrugged. "I guess talking is one thing and feeling is another. You'd better go after her. I need to think, anyway."

Toby looked doubtful. But Jane was certainly more upset than Andy. So she told her roommate she'd see her later and left.

Alone in the room, Andy heaved a sigh of relief. She'd told Toby the truth. She *did* need to think. She'd taken Step One by following

Gigi and finding the things in the broom closet. Now what was Step Two?

Dismissing the possibility of using the clothes and wig to trap Gigi, she focused on the only other item she'd found. Of course! The tape recorder. Perfect!

Dark eyes gleaming, she got down on her knees and thumbed through the cassettes for her own tape recorder. Selecting one by a well-known rock group, she got up and hurried to the door. Checking first to make sure the hall was empty, she ran to the broom closet, hiding the cassette in the folds of her sweatshirt.

Inside the little room, she went straight to Gigi's tape recorder. Pressing down on the Eject button, she removed the music box tape and installed her own. Before she replaced the recorder in its hiding place, she turned the Volume button as high as it would go. She was grinning impishly when she left the broom closet.

On her way outside to enjoy the day, a treat she felt she'd earned, she wondered if they'd see any positive results that night from her actions. Would Gigi use the recorder? She wouldn't check the tape first, would she? Or the volume? If she doesn't, she thought with satisfaction, all I have to do is lie in wait for her. When good old rock and roll starts blasting across the fourth floor, she'll come running to wherever she hid the tape recorder. And I'll be waiting for her!

"Hey, where have you been?" Matt asked when she joined him on the lawn. The campus was once again crowded with students. But the treasured sunshine was diminishing, nearly hidden by a thick layer of clouds advancing across the sky.

"I didn't know you were out here," Andy replied, giving him a quick kiss on the cheek. "I was just . . . studying some music, that's all!"

When they all returned from dinner later that day, Andy stayed out in the hall, telling her roommates she was going to the broom closet. Thinking that she needed some private time, no one argued with her or asked any questions she wasn't ready to answer.

She didn't go to the broom closet. The place she wanted to be was in the hall. No one even noticed her as she slid behind the potted palm. She wasn't sure just exactly how Gigi planted the tape recorder. Did she hide it, turn it on, and then run? Or did she hide it early in the day, leave it, and then come back later to push the On button? Andy had hoped to catch Gigi in the act of hiding the machine. But the crowd presented a problem. She wouldn't be able to spot someone hiding a *truck* in the after-dinner crowd.

She strained to see over the heads of her classmates. It was no use. But did it really matter? Wherever the recorder might be, sooner or later, Gigi would have to come out of hiding and push the On button. Andy would catch her then.

The crowd thinned, and she tried to relax, leaning against the wall behind the palm. People came and went during the next hour, but no one noticed her.

Her back was beginning to ache and she was wondering if she should forget the whole thing when Gigi Norton emerged from Agnes's room, alone. Andy frowned. She knew for a fact that Agnes had signed out for the evening. Gigi had nothing in her hands but a long, thin white envelope. Andy swallowed her disappointment, telling herself that the tape recorder could already be hidden somewhere. Gigi went straight to the mail slot at the end of the hall, near Room 407.

Nothing sinister about that, Andy thought glumly. It's no crime to mail a letter, although I *am* surprised that she has anyone to write to.

But she jerked to attention as Gigi stuck the envelope through the slot, hesitated a moment, then whirled and *raced* away. Andy stood up straight, holding her breath. No one *ran* from a perfectly harmless mail slot.

Gigi had just managed to disappear into Agnes's room when rock music blasted into the hall, shaking the fourth-floor walls and putting a delighted grin on Andrea Cord's face.

CHAPTER FOURTEEN

Andy was so excited, she was shaking. Seeing Gigi Norton throw open the door to Agnes's room and race down the hall, face scarlet, to the mail slot, was better than getting an A-plus on a tough exam. I've got her now, she thought gleefully. Gigi must have wedged the tape recorder in the mail slot earlier in the day, probably when the hall had been so crowded after dinner. The letter she had just mailed had been her opportunity to push the recorder's On button before racing back to her room. Andy giggled, recalling the shock on Gigi's face when instead of the mellow strains of "The Skaters Waltz," rock and roll crashed down on her.

Other students, including Toby and Jane, poured out of their rooms to find the source of the rock music. Andy could hardly wait to see the expressions on their faces when they saw the result of her detective work. She ran down the hall to join the crowd at the mail slot.

But before she could open her mouth to utter the word she'd been dying to say all day, which was, "Aha!", Gigi pulled the recorder out of the mail slot and said, "Well, my goodness, will you look at this!" She pushed the Off button. The sudden silence seemed as stunning as the first bars of the rock tune had been. "Someone," Gigi continued, eyes wide with innocence, "hid this tape recorder in here. And you know what?"

Andy noticed angrily that the crowd was hanging on Gigi's every word. How could they be so gullible?

"You know what?" Gigi repeated, obviously relishing the attention. "This must be where that music box melody was coming from. The one everyone heard at night after lights out?" She laughed, a shrill sound. "I guess whoever has been playing this little joke didn't get enough attention from such a quiet tape. So tonight, she decided to try something really outrageous."

Andy's voice cut through the corridor. "She? Don't you mean *I*, Gigi? You were the only person at the mail slot just before the music started, and you were the first one there after it started."

"Oh, Andy, so what? With music that loud, anyone who isn't deaf as a post could figure out exactly where it was coming from."

"I repeat, Gigi, you were the *only* person in the hall *before* the music began. I saw you pretend to mail a letter. I suppose that's when you pushed the On button of the recorder you hid earlier." There, that should do it. Gigi couldn't deny she'd been the only one in the hall.

There was a glint in Gigi's pale eyes, but it wasn't one of defeat. "First of all," she said coolly, "obviously, I wasn't the only one in the hall. If you saw me mail my letter, that means you were here, too."

"I was way down at the other end of the hall," Andy said hotly. "Nowhere near the mail slot. There was only you, Gigi. No one else."

Gigi's eyes opened very wide. "Why, Andy," she said smoothly, "just because you didn't *see* anyone else doesn't mean there wasn't anyone there."

The implication was clear and Andy groaned inwardly as girls turned to each other and began whispering excitedly. Any other time, Andy knew, Gigi's flimsy explanations wouldn't have worked. But the atmosphere at Canby Hall was perfect now for her sly hints. The ghost had been on everyone's mind for days.

Someone in the crowd did call out, "Kind of a strange ghost, don't you think, Gigi? Where did it learn to operate a tape recorder?" But the question was drowned out by the loud chattering of girls who didn't want any questioning. They wanted to keep their ghost.

"You *guys!*" Andy shouted in disgust, "Think a minute! There wasn't any ghost. There was only Gigi. Honest!"

But it was hopeless. No one was listening. Everyone had gathered around Gigi — who was entertaining them with *her* version of how the tape recorder got into the mail slot. "She must have put the tape recorder in there over a week ago. Then she just floated by and turned it on every night."

Seeing the expressions on her classmates' faces, Andy didn't even bother to ask rudely how the rock music had found its way into the tape recorder. No one seemed to care.

Disgusted, she returned to her room. She sat down heavily on her bed, staring at the floor. Now what? After all her planning . . . she hadn't chased away the ghost, after all. She'd just made matters worse. When people began to believe someone like Gigi Norton, the campus was really in trouble.

But when Jane and Toby returned, Andy got a surprise. Andy expected Jane to say, "See? I told you Julia Canby was right here on this campus!" But she said nothing of the kind. She said instead, "Okay, I give up. You were right all along. Gigi's behind the whole thing."

Andy's mouth dropped open. "I was? You mean it?"

"Sure." Jane nodded. "I may have gone a bit overboard because of the diary, Andy, but I'm not stupid. Julia wouldn't play rock music." A look of disapproval crossed her face. "She was much too genteel."

"Genteel?" Andy grinned. "Is that because she's gentry?"

Jane laughed. Toby did, too. "Yes," Jane said, "it's because she's gentry. The point is," she added seriously, "I knew the minute I heard that tape that you'd put it there. It's one of your favorites. So when you said the recorder was Gigi's and that she'd hidden it there, I knew you were telling the truth, that you'd proved it somehow." Her shoulders slumped slightly. "Or tried to. It should have worked. And I'm sorry I didn't help at all. I should have listened when you told us what you'd found in the broom closet."

Andy thought for a minute. Then she glanced sideways at Jane. "The *minute* you heard the tape? You believed me the minute you heard that music?" A grin was tugging at her lips.

Jane laughed. "Well, almost. I guess there was a second or two there when I thought maybe Julia's taste in music had changed drastically. But it didn't last. Honest!"

"Andy," Toby asked, "why didn't you go get the clothes and wig? Wouldn't that have helped prove Gigi was the ghost?"

Andy shook her head. "It wouldn't have

proved anything. You saw that innocent act of hers. She would have said that anyone could have put those things in the broom closet. And I didn't have any way of proving that *she* had."

"But we know it was her," Jane said solemnly. She jumped up and began marching back and forth. "Oh, I could just shake her! Of all the rotten, conniving . . . I can't believe I let myself be taken in like that. I mean, how stupid can a person get?"

Andy could see that Jane was very close to tears. Having her roommate back in her corner erased Andy's earlier resentment. "Not your fault," Andy said firmly. "Don't forget, you weren't the only one. Practically the whole school was seeing Julia in every little nook and cranny."

"We saw what Gigi wanted us to see," Toby said. "I guess that's the part that makes me the maddest. She must have been laughing behind our backs that whole time."

"Ooh!" Jane cried, "I can't stand it! The thought of Gigi getting away with this makes me crazy!"

"There's still one thing I just don't get," Andy said, frowning. "The day that I saw Julia, I saw Gigi, too. She couldn't possibly have changed clothes. There wasn't time. How do we explain that?"

It was Jane who gave her the answer. "I think I know," she said, stopping to look at her roommates. "You wouldn't let me finish the other day, Andy, but I started to tell you about Gigi's new friend, Agnes Pearl, from down the hall. Jane paused dramatically. "Agnes looks a lot like Julia. She wouldn't even need the wig, because she has long, dark hair."

Andy stared up at her. "You mean there were *two* of them masquerading as Julia?"

Jane nodded. "I think so. It makes perfect sense. Gigi probably knew we'd suspect her, sooner or later. So she covered her tracks by using Agnes part of the time, and then making sure that one of us saw her at the same time. And she's been using Agnes's room as a base of operations here!"

A sharp knock on the door interrupted them. "Hey, in there!" the voice of their hall monitor called, "It's past lights out. Kill the Thomas Edisons, okay?"

"Listen," Andy said quietly as she switched off the overhead light, leaving on only a small table lamp, "we'd better table this discussion for now. But tomorow after classes, we have to figure out how to cook Gigi's goose, okay?"

Jane and Toby nodded. As angry as she was, Jane was really too tired to think clearly. And Toby was simply sick of wrestling with the problem. "Maybe if we get a good night's sleep," she said, crawling under her bedspread, "the cobwebs will leave our brains and we'll come up with a brilliant plan."

"That sounds familiar," Andy said as she turned off the table lamp. "I told Matt *I* was going to do just that." She laughed, a short, mirthless sound. "Boy, was I ever wrong!"

"Nobody's perfect," Toby muttered, curling up under her blankets, her eyes already closed. "And at least you tried."

"Uh-huh," Jane agreed sleepily. "So go to sleep. We'll talk about it tomorrow."

CHAPTER FIFTEEN

The next day, to Jane's delight, her literature teacher excused her from class. "You can use the time to work on your essay," she said. "That's more important right now than Edgar Allan Poe. Go ahead, scram!"

Jane needed no additional urging. Her essay about Julia was coming along nicely, but she could use the extra time for it. Thanking her teacher, she left class and went straight to the library. It had stopped raining, and the sun was busy drying things out. The air smelled wonderful, and, remembering that they *were* going to do something about Gigi, Jane felt more relaxed than she had in a long time.

Penny Vanderark was already in the library, hunched over a table in the corner, chewing on a pen and frowning furiously. She looked up when Jane came in and relief washed over her face.

"Oh, Jane, thank goodness! Maybe you can help me with my essay. I'm stuck!"

"What's the problem?" Jane sat down, glancing anxiously toward the glass case housing the exhibit. She didn't have that much extra time. She hoped all Penny wanted was a pencil sharpened.

That wasn't what Penny wanted. "I don't know what to write about!" she wailed. "I can't think of a single thing. I know you and I are in competition with each other, but I really need your help. Couldn't you just give me one tiny little idea?"

Jane was annoyed. Didn't she have enough on her mind? Penny had a lot of nerve. But she seemed so sure Jane would help . . . and weren't they all in this together? And it was a little flattering to be asked for help.

"Okay. What kind of essay do you want to write?"

"A serious one." Penny's tone of voice was very definite. "Most of the stuff I've written for the school magazine has been really light. I know everyone thinks I'm an airhead, so — "

"Everyone doesn't," Jane pointed out. "You're up for the Award, aren't you? They don't nominate airheads for awards, Penny."

Penny blushed. "Well, anyway, I want to do a good job just to prove that I'm *not* an airhead. But," her tone became mournful again, "my brain feels like sawdust. I'm totally blank!"

"Well," Jane said, thinking as the words came out, "why don't you write about what's been going on here?"

Penny's blue eyes opened very wide. "You mean write about the ghost?"

Jane nodded. "Sure. That's a serious subject. You could write about how easily intelligent people can get carried away." As her thoughts gathered momentum, so did her words. "And about what happens when they do. You could write about how distracted, even hysterical, people can get when they're not thinking rationally. You remember the story *The Emperor's New Clothes*, don't you? When all the people pretended the king really was wearing a great new outfit, until a little kid piped up and said that he wasn't wearing anything at all? Isn't that a little bit like what happened here?"

"I guess so," Penny answered doubtfully.

Jane sighed with annoyance. Penny might want to write a serious paper, but she certainly wasn't the deepest thinker Jane had ever met. "We *wanted* to believe we saw Julia," she explained patiently, "so we did. Even though we knew better."

"Well, that's serious, all right," Penny said. "Do you really think I can do a good job?"

"You wouldn't have been selected for the essay contest if you couldn't do a good job. Now, I've got to work on my own essay, okay? And listen, Penny, make it serious if you really want to, but personally, I think something funny makes things easier to read, so don't leave the humor out completely, okay?"

"Sure. Listen, thanks a lot, Jane. It was really sweet of you to help. Good luck with your own essay. I'm sure it'll be wonderful." Penny got up and headed for the card catalogues for research material.

Jane smiled as she marched over to collect the diary. She seldom thought of herself as sweet. But it did make her feel good to see Penny so pleased.

Settled in her favorite chair by the window, diary in hand, Jane said good-bye to the Julia Canby invented by Gigi Norton as a prank. *That* Julia Canby had never existed. *But this one,* she thought, patting the diary, *did exist.* And I want to make her come alive in my essay. I owe her that much, because she's taught me a lot. And from now on, whenever I'm having a hissy fit over some silly rule or regulation of my parents or the teachers here at Canby, I'll try hard to remember what Julia's short life was like, packed so full of restrictions and conventions that she must never have felt the sort of freedom *I* feel.

Jane tapped her pen against her teeth. And I'll try to remember, she vowed, even when Toby and Andy and Dee and Maggie and the others are driving me bananas, how lucky I am to be surrounded by friends. I'm almost never lonely, thank goodness! Poor Julia. She had such a good sense of humor, and she hardly ever got to use it.

And, Jane thought sadly as she bent to begin her work, if I forget all of that, maybe I'll at least always remember the most important thing of all: that whatever else is wrong with my life, at least I've still *got* it!

With tears in her eyes, she wrote, "In a bleak and rainy London in the year eighteen ninety-seven, a young girl stood at a hotel room window, looking out over a strange, exciting city."

While Jane wrote, Andy left her dance class early to visit the Drama Department. Although she had no doubts at all about Gigi Norton's role in The Great Ghost Caper, it couldn't hurt to check out a few additional details. The more evidence they had, the less chance there would be that Gigi, who lied as easily as most people breathed, would slide out from under their accusations.

"Yeah, sure, I remember," the student-clerk in Wardrobe told Andy. "I was here last year. We did *The Importance of Being Ernest* in March. What do you need to know about it?"

"I was wondering if you still had the costumes."

The thin girl with thick glasses and short, dark hair nodded. "Yeah, we never get rid of anything. Can't afford to. At this school, the science budget is bigger than the drama budget. So we hang on to everything. A nip here, a tuck there, maybe a dye job in the washing machine, and we can use it again. Which outfit are you interested in?"

"The female lead's," Andy answered without hesitation. "Maroon dress, black cape, wasn't it?" There was nothing going on in this department this late in the year, so except for the two of them, the backstage area, dimly-lighted, was empty. "At least we won't be bothering anyone while we hunt for it," Andy added cheerfully.

"Oh, no hunting," the girl said just as cheerfully. "Everything is catalogued and kept in its own little place. That's my job. It's absolutely essential when you have as much stuff as we have." She began walking toward a wall of floor-to-ceiling cupboards. "Now, let's see . . . ah, here we are!"

Andy wasn't the least bit surprised to find the lock on the cupboard jimmied open and its contents gone. But the clerk was. "Oh, no!" she moaned, "Am I ever in trouble now!" She looked at Andy in dismay. "It's my job to take care of these things. It's one of the responsibilities that comes with my scholarship. What am I going to do? How will I explain this?" Her face reddened. "And if I get my hands on the sneaky rat who did this . . ."

"Let me do that for you," Andy said, grinning. "Relax. It's okay. I just wanted to make sure I wasn't wrong about something. I wasn't.

And you'll have your costume back by tomorrow, I promise."

The girl knew Andy, and trusted her. The panic left her eyes. "Okay, if you say so." She knew Andy hadn't taken the costume, and there was something about Andy's attitude that guaranteed its return.

"Thanks for your help," Andy told her. "And remember, by tomorrow your worries will be over. So take it easy."

She left the Drama Department still smiling and was on her way to her last class of the day when her housemother came out of the library and called to her. "Andy, wait a minute!"

Andy turned. She hoped whatever Merrie wanted wouldn't take long. She had planned to spend her time in English class dreaming up ways to set a trap for weasel Norton.

"Andy," Merrie said as they met at the library entrance, "I need to ask you about something. I was going to come to your room later, but this is better, just the two of us."

Andy frowned. That sounded so mysterious.

"Andy, have you heard any rumors about . . . well, about . . ." Merrie was too embarrassed to complete the question.

"About a ghost?" Andy finished for her.

Merrie's face flushed. "I feel so silly saying it. But obviously you *have* heard something. Why wasn't I told?"

"For the same reason that *you* were embarrassed just now," Andy answered honestly.

"None of us could imagine coming to you and saying, 'Gee, Merrie, we've got this ghost problem.'"

Merrie looked stern. "You girls know you can come to me with anything."

Andy grinned. "Even this?"

"Well . . . if it upsets the whole campus, yes. Especially now, right before finals. Exactly what *is* going on, anyway?"

Andy leaned against a tree and filled her in.

When Andy had finished, Meredith looked bewildered. "I don't understand why I never knew any of this. How on earth were you girls able to study?"

"It wasn't easy," Andy admitted. "I got pretty worried. I could just see Baker House floating in a sea of Fs."

Her housemother shuddered. "So you think one of the students is behind all of this nonsense?"

Andy nodded. "But we have no proof. So that's the next step."

Merrie looked interested. "Any ideas?"

"Uh-uh. Not yet. We're going to huddle after classes today, see what we can come up with." Her eyes sparkled. "Something brilliant, no doubt."

"Are you girls sure you can handle this by yourselves?"

"Well, if we can't, we'll come to you," Andy promised. "But we'd really like a crack at this before we call in reinforcements, okay?"

Her housemother nodded. "Okay. Just be careful, please. If everyone's been as upset by all of this as you say they have, we don't want to add to that."

"Don't worry. There's only one person we want to upset and believe me, she has it coming to her! Now, I've got to get to class. I'll fill you in later." With a good-bye wave, Andy hurried off to class to make final plans to trap Gigi.

CHAPTER SIXTEEN

Andy, Toby, and Jane gathered in Room 407 immediately after classes. Jane's spirits had improved noticeably. All that remained of her earlier mood was the anger toward Gigi and her determination to put an end to the girl's prank. Toby and Andy shared that determination.

"So," Andy said as they settled on their beds armed with snacks and sodas, "who's got a brilliant idea?"

No answer. Toby and Jane munched silently.

"Okay, then, let's think while we feed our faces. We need to come up with something fast. Merrie's upset about all the fuss, and in the dining hall at lunch all I heard was, 'Julia Canby, Julia Canby.' I felt like screaming, 'Gigi Norton, Gigi Norton,' but I bit my tongue. Because after last night, I knew no one would believe me until I had some proof."

Her roommates nodded silently and continued munching.

Toby was the first to make a suggestion. "We know where she hides the costume. We could put glue or spiders inside the clothes. Then, when she puts them on and screams, we could run in and snap her picture."

Andy shook her head. "I'm sure the clothes aren't there anymore. She probably moved them last night after lights out."

"We could corner that Agnes person," Jane offered, "and make her tell us about their nasty little plan."

"She probably wouldn't tell us. Gigi would never forgive her, and Agnes must know that. But . . ." Andy sat up straight, "maybe you've got something there. Not about Agnes, though. She won't tell. But maybe Gigi will!"

Toby stared at her. "Gigi? Are you kidding? Gigi won't tell. She won't admit anything!"

And Jane added dryly, "Getting Gigi to confess would be about as easy as passing our finals blindfolded."

"No, no, no," Andy protested, raising her hands. "I'm not talking about *asking* her to tell the truth. Good grief, I know better than that!" She lowered her voice and her hands. "I was thinking of a little subtle persuasion."

Jane stared, then giggled. "Andy. Subtlety is *not* one of your talents."

Andy tossed her head. "Well, it will be this time. It's the only thing that will work."

A grin began to tug at the corners of Toby's mouth. "Speak English, Andy. When you say subtle persuasion, don't you mean setting Gigi up?"

"Of course!" Andy admitted cheerfully. "That's exactly what I mean."

A knock on the door interrupted them. The door opened and in poked Maggie's curly brown head. "Hi," she whispered. "We think we know what you're up to and we want in, okay?"

The three roommates exchanged quick glances before nodding and waving Maggie inside. She was followed closely by Dee. Closing the door after them, they took places on the floor beside Jane's bed.

"So what's going on?" Dee asked. "You *are* going to blitz this Gigi-ghost business, aren't you?"

"You believed me last night?" Andy said in surprise.

Maggie nodded. "Sure, we did. You wouldn't lie."

"But Gigi would," Dee added. "And we knew you wouldn't let her keep it up. So we figured you'd be conducting a strategy session right about now. I hope you don't mind our butting in."

"Glad you're here." Toby looked grim for a second. "We need all the help we can get.

And you're right — we're *not* going to let Gigi run around campus pretending to be Julia Canby. We're just deciding now how to cut her off at the pass."

"So what are the suggestions so far?" Maggie wanted to know. She was wearing red shorts and top and looked bright and cheerful. It suited her personality.

Andy grinned. "Well, it just so happens I was thinking about fighting fire with fire."

"How?" Jane asked.

"Well," Andy said, "Gigi used a tape recorder, didn't she? Maybe we should take a lesson from her." She was thinking as she talked. "We can use your notes, Jane. Your diary notes." She outlined the details of her plan and then sat back, waiting for their reaction. "Well? What do you think? Bad idea? Good idea? What?"

"Not a good idea," Jane said soberly.

Andy looked like someone had just refused her invitation to a party.

Then Jane grinned. "A terrific idea!"

"Yeah? Really?"

"Sure. Right, guys?" Jane looked around the room. Toby, Dee, and Maggie nodded vigorously, calling, "Sure! Sounds great to us!"

"Great! Let's get going. We've got lots to do."

It took them less than an hour to begin putting their plan in action. They were almost finished when the telephone in their room, on which they could get incoming calls, rang. "It's for you, Toby," Jane announced a moment later. "It's Neal."

Toby took the telephone and glanced around the room shyly. "Um . . . you guys, would you mind?"

They got the message. Getting up, her roommates and neighbors said they'd wait for her outside of Baker House. "Just don't take forever," Andy warned as they left. "Remember, we've got important business to take care of."

Toby nodded. Then she picked up the phone, saying softly, "Hi, Neal. How are things in Boston?"

"Fine. But I miss you."

Toby smiled. Neal's deep voice always made her feel warm all over. It was easy to picture his strong square face and deep blue eyes, the neatly-styled blond hair waving across his forehead. It had been much too long since she'd last seen him!

"So I was wondering if the invitation to your class dinner was still good."

He had said he couldn't make it. She had almost asked Randy Crowell, a friend of hers who lived on a nearby farm. Then she'd decided that if she couldn't have Neal there, she didn't want anyone. "Of course it still stands. You mean you can come?"

"Well, I'm *going* to. I'll just double up on

my work load, that's all." His voice softened. "I need to see you."

She wasn't going to argue with that. She knew his studies were important to him. Neal was very bright. That was one of the things she really liked about him. It was also one of the reasons she didn't see him as often as she would have liked. Neal planned to be a lawyer, and said the competition in his field was "fierce." At least her competition wasn't another girl.

"I need to see you, too," she said quietly. "And I'm really glad you're coming to the dinner. I'm sure Jane's going to win the Lit Award. It'll be extra-nice for her if you're here, too."

Jane and Neal had known each other all their lives. Their parents, who were good friends, had expected them to marry one day. But then Jane had met Cary. And Neal had been introduced to October Houston. But Jane and Neal were still friends, and Toby knew she was telling the truth when she said that Jane would be pleased by his presence at the Awards Banquet.

"Listen," she said, "I've gotta go, Neal," remembering the group waiting outside for her. "Something really crucial is going on. I'll tell you all about it when I see you, okay? I can't wait!"

When she had replaced the receiver, she hurried downstairs.

"Well, I'm glad *somebody's* working on her romance," Andy said as Toby ran down Baker House's stone steps. "I feel like I always thought I'd feel if I went to an all-girls school! It's like I live on an all-female planet! The only time I see Matt these days is when we're studying." She made a face of disgust. "Not exactly the ideal date, is it?"

"Better than nothing!" Dee said laughing.

"Dee," Andy said, shaking her head, "you haven't spent a Friday or Saturday night alone since the guys at Oakley Prep discovered your existence."

They were all laughing as they entered the dining hall. While Andy and Jane left the group to tend to the first step of their scheme, the others got on line. Toby located Gigi Norton right away. Bumping Dee's elbow with her own, she said, "Look, there she is. Over there at that table. She's with Agnes!"

"Agnes *does* look a little like Julia Canby," Dee whispered, "but she's not as pretty." Maggie nodded agreement.

"I'm sure we were right," Toby added, placing a dinner roll and a carton of milk on her tray. "It was both of them, working together. If Andy hadn't figured it out, they'd probably go right on doing it."

"Yeah," Dee agreed as they moved forward in the line, "and Jane would go right on being so preoccupied with ghostly things, she'd probably lose the Lit Award to Gigi."

"Which," Maggie said, "is almost certainly what Gigi had on her little bitty mind from the beginning."

Trays full, they took their seats at a table where Gigi would be in their line of vision. Jane returned, a secretive smile on her lips as she quickly filled a tray and joined them. "Andy will be here in a minute," she said cheerfully as she sat down. "She . . ." glancing in Gigi's direction, "had something really important to do." But Gigi gave no sign that she'd heard.

Penny Vanderark came in before Andy returned. In excited whispers, Dee and Maggie filled her in on their plan.

"Oh, that's great!" she whispered back. "I wouldn't miss this for anything. I can't wait to see the look on her face!"

"I think she knows we're up to something," Toby warned in a low voice. "She keeps looking over here and she's as nervous as a butterfly in a cactus patch. We'd better cool it, or we'll give the whole thing away."

They calmed down, and moments later a flushed Andy ran into the dining room. Jane held her breath. Would it work? It had to!

Andy slid into a seat just as a voice came over the P. A. system, surprising everyone. The voice was clear and the words carefully spoken in cultivated tones. If the voice itself wasn't startling, the words were:

"This is Julia Canby." Everyone stopped

eating and drinking. All eyes turned toward the loudspeaker.

"Look shocked!" Andy hissed at her companions. They obeyed. Then they all sneaked a peek in Gigi's direction. Stiffling a giggle, Toby whispered, "My goodness, the girl is as white as a . . . ghost?" Everyone around her who knew what was going on had to choke back a giggle.

The voice on the P.A. system continued: "Gigi? Gigi Norton? I wish to speak to Gigi Norton, please."

Every last ounce of color drained from Gigi's face.

"You sound great, Andy!" Jane whispered. "What an actress! She couldn't possibly recognize your voice."

"You will think this strange, I know, Gigi Norton, but I feel a strong kinship to you and felt the need to speak directly to you, just this once. We do look a bit alike, do we not? Perhaps you are the sister I always wished for and never had. I want you to know that I, too, get lonely and wish for companionship. I have spent many lonely afternoons in London, sitting on the windowseat in my room, watching the rain stream down the window."

Gigi was furiously biting her lower lip. Everyone else listened in rapt attention.

"You know what that feels like, don't you, Gigi? Being alone, I mean? I sense that in you. There were those days in London when

Mathilde, my maid, was busy elsewhere, and I had only the sound of the rain to keep me company. And the day when Edward Lynch came to visit and Papa threw him out, I was desolate. I have this feeling that you would understand my misery that day, Gigi.

"I wish we could have been friends. I didn't have many. I can only tell you that if I *had* had them, I would have been very careful to be kind to them always. Are you kind to your friends, Gigi?"

Jane made a disgusted sound low in her throat. Andy shot her a warning look and Jane shrugged.

"I must go now, Gigi. You are a special person. Remember, be kind . . . be kind. . . ."

The voice faded away. The P.A. system crackled briefly and then there was silence in the room.

"Clever idea," Dee murmured to Andy, "making it a friendly message. If you'd attacked her or accused her of anything, she would have known we were behind it. Look at her face. She looks like she's going to pass out any second now."

Everyone waited for Gigi to say something. Nervous whispers and giggles escaped as all heads turned toward her.

"That was Julia Canby," she finally whispered. Then she repeated it, more loudly this time.

Andy shrugged. "Yeah? So what? We've

been hearing from her for a long time now. What's the big deal?"

"No," Gigi protested, "you don't understand. That was *her!*"

"I don't think it was," Jane said flatly. "I think you taped that message yourself. No one else would say anything nice about you."

Gigi got to her feet, swaying slightly. "Will you *listen?*" she cried in a shrill voice. "I'm telling you that wasn't me this time."

Andy stood up, too. "Not this time?" she asked gently.

Gigi shook her head. "No," she began babbling, "I don't even know all that stuff about Julia, so how could I say those things? Maybe it was me before, but I had nothing to do with this message!"

Andy picked up on her remarks, raising her own voice. "Maybe it was you before? What does that mean? You mean that was you wearing the Victorian clothes, wearing that wig, scaring people? That was you playing the music box tune?"

Gigi hesitated for just a second before admitting, "Yes. Yes, that was me."

CHAPTER SEVENTEEN

The only sound in the dining hall was the whirring of the overhead ceiling fans.

"Would you like to repeat that?" Andy asked softly.

"Yes! Yes, I would! I said I *did* do the other things. Agnes helped," glancing down at her companion, who flushed and looked away. "But I *didn't* make that message just now over the P.A. system. It had to be Julia."

Andy smiled and sat down. "Oh, Gigi, don't be silly. You know perfectly well there are no such things as ghosts. How could you have thought for a minute that Julia Canby was actually talking to you? Why, my goodness, Gigi, she's been dead for years!"

"But . . . but if it wasn't Julia, then who?"

Andy smiled again. Jane and Toby and Dee and Maggie and Penny allowed very large grins of triumph to spread across their faces.

160

As excited as Gigi was, those grins were impossible to miss. Or to misinterpret.

"I . . . I didn't recognize the voice in the message," she said. "That's why I thought it was Julia." But her voice was losing conviction as she continued to stare at the triumphant faces gazing at her. Beginning to panic, she glanced around the room. Her eyes met one hostile stare after another. Finally, she brought her gaze back to Andy.

Gigi sagged against the table. "You . . . you did this. That was *your* voice on the tape." Then her body jerked upright again. "You *tricked* me!" Her pale face flamed with spots of bright red color. "Of all the nasty . . ."

"Yes," Andy replied calmly, getting to her feet again, "it's my voice. At least I had a better reason than you did to pull that kind of stunt. I wanted to get at the truth. What's *your* excuse?"

Everyone in the room stared at Gigi, waiting for her answer. She said nothing, her eyes on Andy in a furious stare.

"When P.A. finds out that you were behind all of this nonsense," Jane told Gigi in a cold voice, "you'll wish you *were* a ghost."

Murmurs of agreement circulated throughout the dining hall.

"Are you going to tell her?" Gigi asked stiffly. "I was just having a little fun. If you tell her, I'll be expelled.

"You weren't just having fun," Jane hissed

angrily. "You were trying to blitz everyone else's chances of winning that Lit Award by shaking up the whole campus. And you almost succeeded. We ought to tar and feather you. That's probably what they would have done when Julia Canby was alive."

"We'll have to think about it," Andy told Gigi in a nonchalant voice. Turning away, she said to Jane in a low voice, "Let her worry about it for a while. She deserves to worry."

When they left, Gigi was still standing at her place, surrounded by angry classmates.

"Maybe that's punishment enough," Toby suggested as they walked toward Baker House. "Everyone knows now that she was behind the ghost business. And they all hate her for fooling them like that. We'd probably be doing her a favor if we got her expelled."

Jane shook her head. "I don't think we should tell P.A. If I were responsible for getting any student, even one as miserable as Gigi Norton, expelled from Julia Canby's school, I think my dreams really would be haunted. Gigi was never very popular, and now she'll be lucky if she can get a *teacher* to speak to her. Toby's right, that's punishment enough."

Andy thought for a few minutes. "Well, I'll agree to that," she said finally, "only if certain persons of Room 407 and friends make absolutely certain that Gigi Norton does *not* walk off with that Lit Award. That would just be too much! How about it, Jane? Penny?"

Jane nodded vehemently. "There is no way," she said deliberately, "that Gigi is going to take that Award. I promise you that!"

"You know," Dee said thoughtfully, "if you did tell P.A. about Gigi's trickery, I'll bet she'd disqualify her from the essay contest. You and Penny wouldn't have to worry about her anymore."

"No!" Surprised by her own vehemence, Jane lowered her voice. "No. I'd rather win fair and square and I'm sure Penny would, too, wouldn't you, Penny?"

"Yes. Anyway, I'm not worried about Gigi's essay. It'll probably be as mean and small-minded as she is. And," Penny added happily, "thanks to Jane's idea, my own essay is turning out pretty well."

Andy looked interested. "Oh, yeah? Has Jane been handing out advice again?"

Penny smiled at Jane. "*Good* advice. And it's working. But I'm not telling anybody what it's about until I'm finished. You'll all just have to wait and see."

"Speaking of finishing," Jane commented as she opened the door to Baker House, "now that we've punched a hole in Gigi's nasty scheme, I've got to tackle the finishing touches on my own essay. There isn't much time left."

So, although their efforts to unveil Gigi's treachery had left them all drained, they spent the evening studying. And, for the first time in a long while, the only music accompanying their studies was their own.

One afternoon shortly before the class dinner, Jane was summoned to the office of Canby Hall's President, Patrice Allardyce. So nervous her fingernails tingled, Jane stopped in front of the big antique desk, clasped her hands behind her back, and waited. Ms. Allardyce, crisp and efficient-looking in a blue and white two-piece dress, stood up and came around the desk to greet her.

"Congratulations!" she said, extending her hand. "Your wonderfully creative essay about our founder's daughter has won this year's Literature Award for you. That must make you very happy."

Jane's body sagged with relief. It was finally finished, all of it, and she had won! She shook Ms. Allardyce's hand. "Thank you," she said breathlessly, "thank you."

"I'm telling you a few days early because there may be people you'd like to invite to your class dinner to see you accept the Award." Ms. Allardyce returned to her desk, leaning against it and facing Jane.

"And I wanted to thank you personally," she said with a smile, "for suggesting to Penny that she follow up on your own essay."

"She told you?"

"Yes. I just spoke with her. Her essay was

very good. It was difficult to decide between the two of you, frankly."

"I'm glad for Penny. I mean I'm glad you liked her essay. I knew she could do it."

"I think you really mean that. By the way, Jane, the two essays together gave us a rather clear picture of the recent situation on campus. And we're grateful to those of you who put an end to all that nonsense."

Jane stared at the headmistress. "You know about that?"

Ms. Allardyce laughed. "I didn't know while it was happening, I must confess. I'm not sure how it all slipped by me. I pride myself on keeping a finger on the pulse of this school. But I suppose end-of-the-year matters were keeping me too preoccupied to notice what was going on. The essays explain it all. Yours and Penny's, I mean."

Meaning, Jane thought, that Gigi didn't mention it in hers. Of course not. Why would she?

"I must say, my admiration for all of you has increased, knowing that you wrote your essays and studied for your finals under such difficult circumstances. It's amazing that you were able to concentrate at all."

"How did you know about our scheme to catch the . . . ghost?" Jane asked. "Penny?"

Ms. Allardyce nodded. "She was in a very good mood. I gather that makes her talkative."

Jane laughed. "Bad moods work the same

way with Penny. Also eating and studying and rainy days and boys and athletic events and . . . well, Penny just likes to talk, that's all. She's very expressive."

"Well," the headmistress said, returning to take a seat behind her desk, "please pass my gratitude on to your . . . associates in this matter. Tell them for me that I appreciate the way you all handled things. Oh, and Jane," she called as Jane turned to leave, "Penny also mentioned that you felt the guilty party shouldn't be expelled. I gave it some thought, and I concur. And I'm happy that none of you is out to seek revenge. Revenge is not an attractive quality in a young woman — or a young man."

"No, of course not, Ms. Allardyce," Jane agreed. "We didn't think expulsion was a good idea, that's all."

"I agree. Run along now. You must have phone calls to make. And Jane . . ."

"Yes?"

"Thank you for a lovely portrait of our founder's young daughter. And you did it all without touching a paintbrush. That's really quite remarkable."

Flushing with pleasure and thanking her headmistress, Jane took her leave. Her feet seemed to be floating above the carpet and her eyes were shining with pride.

Her roommates were overjoyed with the news of her triumph. "That'll get me through finals!" Andy cried with glee. "I knew you could do it."

"Not without you guys, I couldn't have," Jane said, already checking the closet for something super-special to wear to the dinner. "If you'd just ignored the whole thing, I'd still be looking for ghosts on campus."

Andy shook her head. "Not true. You made up your own mind. That night when I tried to catch Gigi planting the recorder, you were the one who decided she was lying and I was telling the truth."

Toby interrupted. "Don't argue about it," she said mildly. "It's all over, thank goodness. Jane, what *are* you doing? You're going through that closet like you were hunting for buried treasure."

"I am. But most of *this* treasure should *be* buried. I simply have to go shopping! Anybody want to join me?"

Since both Andy and Toby also wanted something special to wear to the dinner, they were only too happy to agree to accompany her.

"*After* finals," Andy warned. "We don't have time before then. Let's ask Dee and Maggie and Penny. We'll make an outing out of it. It'll be our reward for acing our tests."

"You sound pretty sure of yourself," Jane said, abandoning the hopeless closet. "I wish I were that sure."

"We are *all* going to whiz through them,"

Andy said with conviction. "After all, they couldn't be that much harder than catching Gigi at her dirty tricks, could they? And we came through that with flying colors!"

Although Jane was excited about the Award, which made it difficult to concentrate on anything else, she made her phone calls with her good news and then settled down to study. An enormous feeling of peace welled up in her. She had finished the essay and it had won. Her parents had been thrilled when she told them. And Cary had congratulated her with great warmth and laughed at her story about how they'd caught Gigi using her own methods of deception. He had even agreed to wear a suit to the dinner.

"Are you sure you'll recognize me?" he'd teased.

"Oh, Cary, don't be silly. Why, I'd know you anywhere!"

The night of the dinner was going to be a grand evening. She could hardly wait.

But wait she did. The time until then, full of finals, preparations for the dinner, and a riotous shopping trip — to Boston — for dresses, passed quickly. And the night of the dinner arrived at last.

"You look absolutely beautiful, Jane," Andy said warmly, looking lovely herself in a bright red dress with thin shoulder straps and a narrow waist above a full, swirling skirt.

Jane's gown was pale blue, trimmed in cream lace at the high neckline and the cuffs of long, full sleeves. "Very Victorian, don't you agree?" she teased. "Think I could pass for Julia Canby?"

"Jane!" Toby, wearing a soft fabric dotted with tiny sprigs of flowers in a tailored dress that suited her, shook her head. "That's not funny. After everything we went through. . . ."

"Sorry. I guess she's just on my mind. Ms. Allardyce asked me to read part of my essay about Julia tonight after I receive the Award. It" — Jane blushed — "it almost seems like she's here tonight, if saying that doesn't make you all hysterical with worry that I'm falling into that trap again."

"No," Andy said kindly, "I know what you mean. And who knows?" She smiled. "Maybe you're right. If someone were going to make a speech praising me, you can bet I'd attend, no matter where I was at the time."

Toby nodded. "If you feel strongly that she's here, Jane, then maybe she is. We can't know that she's not."

"Well," Jane said, picking up a lacy white wrap and tossing it around her shoulders, "I just hope she likes what I have to say about her, then. C'mon, let's go. There are people waiting for us."

And there were. Jane's parents, formally dressed and looking very elegant, were in the lobby downstairs, along with Cary, wearing the promised suit, a white shirt, and a tie, and Matt and Neal, who had arrived only moments before the girls came downstairs.

"Neal!" Toby cried, her eyes lighting up. "You made it."

"Of course I made it," he said, taking several strides that brought him to her side. "Would I miss your class dinner?"

After hugs all around, Jane led everyone but Toby and Neal outside, giving the two of them a few moments alone. "We'll meet you at the dining hall," she called over her shoulder. "Don't dawdle too long!"

Neal would have preferred to dawdle just a bit longer, but Toby was afraid they'd miss something. "I'd die if I missed Jane's Award presentation," she said softly. "We can talk afterward, though." Because it was almost impossible for Neal to tell Toby no, and because she looked unusually beautiful in the flowered dress, he settled for one kiss before letting Toby lead the way to the ceremony.

When Jane and Cary had been seated in the dining hall, she said nervously, "I'm going to forget every word I was going to say."

He laughed. "No, you're not. You won't forget a thing. If I were a politician and you were my opponent in a campaign right now, I'd drop out. And not just because you look beautiful, either, although you do. But because you're smart, or you wouldn't be getting this award in the first place." His thin face looked very serious. "It's very hard to get, you know."

Yes, she knew. And she *was* proud — of herself and of her school. The dining hall looked really pretty, its plain, rustic interior decorated with pastel-colored crepe paper streamers overhead and large, low baskets of flowers on every table. Her parents kept smiling at her, and she knew they were every bit as proud as she was. But that didn't necessarily mean, she knew, that her father could be talked out of his plans for her. Investment banking! How boring! She'd just have to keep working on him.

The awards weren't to be presented until after the meal. Jane was unable to swallow one little bite. Penny, who was being given the Honorable Mention award, had no such problems, and chattered cheerfully throughout the meal. Jane envied Penny her calm. Reminding herself that she had told Ms. Allardyce no one minded Penny's chattering, she tried to ignore it and relax.

The time finally came. The headmistress, splendid in a royal blue gown, gave a brief welcoming and end-of-the-year speech before saying the words Jane had been waiting a long time to hear: "And now, I would like to present the Award for Excellence in the field of Literature to a Baker House resident, Jane Elizabeth Barrett. Jane, would you come up here, please?"

Applause greeted Jane as she stood up. Cary stood up, too, to give her a quick kiss on the cheek. Then Jane walked to the front of the room, cheeks rosy with pleasure, her head held high.

She accepted the award, thanked Ms. Allardyce, and then turned to face her friends and parents and fellow students.

This one's for you, Julia, she thought. Then she took a deep breath and began. "In a bleak and rainy London in the year eighteen ninety-seven, a young girl stood at a hotel room window, looking out over a strange, exciting city."

The audience sat quietly, listening.

Toby and Andy knew better than to let Jane talk them into taking a crazy summer job. But they did! Read The Girls of Canby Hall #26, HELP WANTED!